WHAT THE CHARACTERS IN
MY BROTHER J...

"FIVE STARS for my brother Javi's ... for the dog community, reminding us all how we're nere ... Javi's not only my brother; he's also my superhero."

❖ **Binah, 3-year-old Havanese**

"My best fur friend, Binah, discovers her brother Javi's diary. It's filled with both educational and inspirational messages. Thank you, Javi. I miss you. See you at Starbarks Park, Binah." ❖ **Daisy, 2-year-old Havachon**

"Javi's memoir captures both the human and dog hearts from the day Javi is born to the day he is reborn. Although I would have liked to read more about me, it leaves me hopeful for a sequel."

❖ **Chloe, 1-year-old Tibetan Terrier**

"Socks off to Javi and Binah for this artful tale that answers so many life questions except who's Tracy Stopler and why is her name on the cover of this book? ❖ **Cooper, 2-year-old Cockapoo**

"Javi is a special soul. His story is filled with love, humor, heartbreak, and more love. You will laugh and cry as you discover your own strengths to overcome life's most challenging circumstances. This story will inspire you to rescue a dog or two." • **Dr. Noah, Veterinarian**

"Sweet Javi met our daughter, Tali, at the perfect time. He instantly added joy, spontaneity, and meaning not only to her life, but also to our family's life. Javi single-handedly turned us into dog lovers."

• **Gramma and Grampaw**

"What an honor it has been for me to experience the charm of Javi, who weaves a hypnotic, fairy tale that's strong enough to capture our imagination and transform darkness into light. His wisdom will be shared for generations to come so that the best of him will continue to live in each of us. Thank you, *mi amore*." • **Tali**

"There are no words in any language to describe the love between a dog and his human. If only humans knew with certainty that their beloved best friends remain with them *always* in some way, in some form, for their existence here on Earth. I believe that *now*." ♥ **Javier**

My Brother Javi
A Dog's Tale

Tracy Stopler

Copyright © February 22, 2020 by Tracy Stopler

LIBRARY OF CONGRESS CATALOGING-IN-PUBLICATION DATA
Stopler, Tracy, author
My Brother Javi: A Dog's Tale

ISBN-13:978-1541319431
ISBN-10:1541319435

Printed in the United States of America

Cover Design: Rich Lehan

Cover Photograph by Shutterstock.com
https://www.shutterstock.com/license
SL Digital Image License Code: 682785499

This Book Is Dedicated To

Javi and Binah, the perfect little loves of my life.

(Mommy, please don't leave out our cousins.)

And to
Coco, Annabelle, Cody, Pluto, Molly, Maisie, Riley, and Abby.

(What about our best furever friends?)

Plus
Elvis, Misty, Ali, Daisy, Chloe, and Cooper.

A special shout-out to all the service dogs who partner up with
the brave men and women who serve our country.
Thank you, Duke, Corky, and Loki.

In Loving Memory of
Javi

November 23, 1999–July 23, 2011

We miss you

Grampaw

December 30, 1937–March 13, 2018

My Brother Javi
A Dog's Tale

"No matter how little money
and how few possessions you own,
having a dog makes you rich."

—Louis Sabin

Binah

IF THIS WERE THE BEGINNING OF A MOVIE, HERE'S WHERE THE camera would zoom in on my face, and I'd say, "Not all superheroes wear capes."

I learned this from my favorite superhero of all time, my brother, Javi, a purebred shih tzu. He was a bit sensitive about things, so I must tell you that his breed is pronounced *sheed zoo*, which is Chinese for lion, not *shit sue*, which is English for something less appealing.

While we're on the subject of pronunciation, his nickname is pronounced *JA-vee*. His real name is Java. When he was born, he was the color of coffee with milk, so the humans named him Java, a generic term for coffee.

Javi was a deep thinker, a reader, and a writer. Don't ask how he learned to read and write. Just know that we dogs are smarter than you think.

Way smarter.

When I was just a puppy, Javi told me that human babies choose their mommies before they're born. When I looked confused, he said, "When a soul is in heaven, before it begins its mission on Earth, it chooses a mommy who will be able to provide it with the opportunity to grow and change."

Javi believed that a dog's soul chooses its human in the same way. "The soul of a dog calls out to the soul of a human," he said. In other words, they fall in love, and the human feeds, walks, and cleans up after the dog forever. It's a marriage of sorts, until death do them part.

My name is Binah. I'm a three-year-old Havanese. That's pronounced Have-a-knees. Although Javi and I came from different birth mamas, we're still siblings because we share the same human mommy. Every day for the past three years, our mommy, whose name is Tali, has told me that I'm a dream come true. She starts off with, "Who's my favorite little girl?"

"Me?" I bark.

"Yes, Binah. You are such a good girl. You are beautiful, you are funny, and you are so smart. I love you to pieces."

Oh, how I love to hear those words. I think. *They never get old.*

"And who is my favorite little boy?"

"Javi!" I bark with confidence.

Mommy confirms, "Yes, your brother, Javi. He introduced you to me in a dream. He sent you to me and told me that your name was Binah. Your brother sent me understanding."

Binah means understanding.

4

"Do you remember what language the word *Binah* comes from?"

"Hebrew?" I tilt my head toward the right and then the left.

"That's right. *Binah* means 'understanding' in Hebrew."

"I know. I know. I know," I bark excitedly as my tail wags a thousand beats per minute.

I like to wear dresses, play ball-ball, tell jokes, and read—not just picture books but books with words. Javi even taught me how to turn the pages.

One day while I was exploring the backyard, I discovered parts of Javi's buried treasure—his diary. He wanted me to share it with my friends after he was gone. If we had thumbs, we'd all give Javi's story two thumbs-up because Javi changed us into believers.

We now believe in miracles.

Javi taught me that miracles don't happen in my comfort zone. He also taught me about the importance of friendship and the challenges of change. With the tenderness of a snowflake, the compassion of a saint, and the brain of a really smart human, Javi taught me how to let go of what I no longer needed.

It's now my mission in life to share Javi's story with the world. Even though I didn't officially meet Javi until I was two months old (chapter 28 of this book), I've added a few chapters of my own story about some conversations with my best friends.

It's a great honor for me to share with you *My Brother Javi: A Dog's Tale.*

—*Binah*

This is me wearing my favorite dress.

This is me with my favorite ball-ball.

THE BEGINNING

"Outside of a dog,
a book is man's best friend.
Inside of a dog,
it's too dark to read."

—Groucho Marx

1
Javi

WAS 1999 A GOOD YEAR? YOU BET IT WAS.

In this year, a squeaky carrot was a dog's favorite toy. The popular dog movies included *A Dog of Flanders* starring Patrash, a male Labrador retriever; *Soccer Dog* starring Kimble, who was renamed Lincoln; and *A Dog's Tale* starring a young boy named Tim who is accidentally changed into a German shepherd.

I wondered if the reverse can happen: *Can a dog change into a little boy?*

Young boys and girls read all about Clifford the Big Red Dog, and watched *Scooby-Doo* on TV. Eight-year-old Kirby, a papillon, became the first of his breed to claim the Best-in-Show title at the Westminster Kennel Club Dog Show.

When my mama, who was named Mama, was a puppy she met her first human family. She traveled from Montague Township,

New Jersey, over the Delaware River, and into the small town of Milford, Pennsylvania.

The town of Milford was so small that it had only one zip code, one gas station, one supermarket, and one ice cream store. Humans who wanted to go out to shop for clothes or go out to eat food using knives had to travel six miles into Matamoras or seven miles into Port Jervis.

One winter day a few years later, as Mama made her way through half-frozen slush that formed mini-rivers flowing into the streets, she started to pant heavily.

At that time, my world was dark inside Mama's body. I was suspended in a warm bath with my peaceful sister and my agitated brother who kept saying, "Be afraid." The three of us were cramped together for a total of sixty-three days.

Soon enough, the warm bath emptied, and there was even less space between us. The temperature changed and the coziness was gone. Although I kept my paws to myself, my brother kicked me. Actually, I can't be certain that it was my brother because my eyes were closed. I just know it wasn't my sister because I sensed she was too fragile.

"Be afraid," I heard my brother roar one last time.

The cool air squeezed itself through the small spaces we didn't fill. When it suddenly touched me—yes, the cool air actually touched me and gave me goose bumpy skin—I felt it gently push me. Now, my eyes were closed, but in my mind's eye, I saw this small, bright, white light. It was far away at first. It must've been a magnet because it pulled me toward it. It was a very strong pull.

That's when I whispered to my sister, "Little girls first."

That's what good brothers do, right?

Again, I sensed she was too tired and too scared to inch forward. My brother, on the other hand, was impatient to move toward the light. I gave him an opportunity to squirm past me, but he wouldn't take it. When I tried to wriggle my body to pass him, he kicked me again. Because there was no room to stand up for myself, I opened my mouth to tell him "go." That's when he kicked me a third time, knocking out my tooth and leaving a black "wound of war" birthmark on the tip of my tongue.

Ouch.

The brilliant, magnificent light grew larger and larger until I became a part of it, and as fate would have it, I was born first on November 23, 1999. I was born with the hiccups. Everyone was laughing, including Mama.

Yes, dogs laugh.

Some dogs simply wag their tail; others grin as if they're posing for the camera. Mama's laugh was a rare panting, not the labor kind, but more of a "ha-ha."

In between the laughter, a deep human voice announced, "It's a boy. He's the color of coffee with cream and sugar."

"Let's call him Java," said another voice that was softer.

"No, Daddy. Let's call him Javi," squeaked yet another voice.

"Okay, Sarai." Daddy announced, "Javi it is!"

Sarai squealed, "Mommy, I hope the next puppy's a girl."

Mommy said, "Me too, Sarai. Is there another one, Roger?"

"Yes. There's definitely another one."

They'll soon discover it's another boy, I thought, *black as coal, a mad warrior who had knocked out my tooth.*

"You're doing great, Mama," said Roger. "One more push."

Mama whimpered.

"Is it a girl?" asked Sarai.

"Right now, it's just a white fluffy marshmallow."

"Aw!" Sarai sang out.

The smell of my aggressive brother became fainter and fainter, but his words—*be afraid*—echoed in my head.

"It's a. . . GIRL."

Where did my brother go? I wondered.

"Princess! Princess!" Sarai chanted out.

I froze when big hands picked me up and moved me. I wiggled around until I felt the warmth of Mama. Feeling safe and hungry, I started to feed. Although I couldn't see my sister because my eyes were still closed, I felt her soft, warm body next to me.

"How's Princess Leia for a name?" asked Roger.

Mommy said, "Roger, she's not feeding."

I tried to open my eyes, but they wouldn't budge. Although I couldn't see, I could hear everything. I gathered milk from Mama and spilled it from my mouth into Princess Leia's mouth.

That's what good brothers do! I thought.

Roger called out, "Neha, get me the baby bottle."

My mama said, "Javi, my son, there are two kinds of dogs in this world: givers and takers. A dog who takes your food will get a bellyache. Maybe not right away, but he's destined for it. A dog who gives you food is kind and will receive credit in his next life."

Next life? I thought. *I'm just starting this one.*

My belly quickly warmed as I nursed and snuggled up to Mama.

"You're a good boy, Javi," Mama said. "Always do the right thing, especially when nobody's watching."

"I'll try, Mama."

Sarai kissed me. "Javi, your sister, Princess, is now drinking from the bottle."

I'm so happy, I thought.

Like all puppies, I was born with an instinct to huddle. I nestled my head under Mama's body and licked Princess Leia's fur as my snout touched her snout. I wondered where my brother was. Nobody had mentioned him, not even once.

Suddenly, a weird sensation overcame me. First it danced around in my belly. Then it ran down my body. In a blink of an eye, it—whatever *it* was—escaped out of my tushy with a loud noise. Although I couldn't see it, I could smell it. My nose crinkled involuntarily.

Pee-ew.

The sound of human laughter bounced off the walls.

Sometime later—I didn't know how to keep track of time—Mama said, "Javi, right now your head is overly large for your small body, your nose is too small for the size of your head and your lips are undeniably human. But, you're precious and very lovable." She kissed the tiny nose on my big head. "You'll grow into any imperfections."

"When?"

"When you embrace them."

"Do you like everything about yourself, Mama?"

"Do you see my underbite? I never liked how my lower jaw extends past my upper jaw. It's quite common in our shih tzu breed. Although our teeth come in later than other dogs, they fall out earlier. You'll most likely have the same experience."

"So we're the same, Mama?"

"No, Javi. We're not the same, but we're equal. It's our differences rather than our similarities that make us special."

"Am I special because I had a tooth before I was born?"

"Puppies aren't born with teeth, Javi. What makes you special is the birthmark on your tongue." Mama leaned in very close to me and examined my tongue. "Your birthmark looks like a heart, Javi. You're very lucky because you'll have that forever."

My brother left me with a heart?

I imagined my brother with a flat face. Everything about him was dark, including his thoughts. Although I never saw him, I still felt him.

As my brother, I suppose he'll always be a part of me.

Princess Leia staggered on her legs and bumped into me. I knew she was fragile. I petted her and discovered she had fur like mine.

"I love you, Princess Leia," I said.

She didn't answer me.

Yaaaaawn.

That was a hearty yawn, the kind where I tried to catch enough air for my sister and me. I zigzagged away from Mama, who had just completed her ritual cleaning, to lie down. I soon drifted off to sleep to the sound of Mama singing:

"Sometimes when a puppy yawns,

an angel dog will transform

into a human spirit just reborn.

La-la-la-la-la-de-da."

2
Binah

Hey, it's me again, Binah. So now I know how Javi's story begins. He had never shared that with me.

I was only two months old when I first met Javi and five months old when he told me to take care of Mommy, but more about that later.

Our house was made of stone, just like the other eight houses on the cul-de-sac. Our fenced-in backyard was rectangular and big enough to park twelve of Mommy's cars. Just so you know, Mommy has only one car, but it's big enough to hold ten dogs, not including Javi's friend Elvis, who was a giant.

In our backyard, the white fence ran along both sides and the back of our house, which was the side of Daisy's house. Mommy put a shed in one corner and a koi pond in the shape of a kidney bean in another corner. Large stones surrounding the pond held onto one another like the pieces of a jigsaw puzzle. Although Javi had left to travel over the Rainbow Bridge, his sweet scent still lingered.

It was quiet.

Kind of.

Daisy pushed her way under the fence, as she'd done so many times before, scrambled to her feet, lifted her head, and announced, "Here I am!" Her eyes widened. "Oh my God! Oh my GOD! OH MY GOD!" Daisy barked.

I love Daisy. She's one of my best friends, but she can be such a drama queen.

We saw each other often. Whenever Mommy went away, I stayed with Daisy, and whenever Daisy's family went away, she stayed with us. At our house, it was just Mommy, me, and the fishies. At Daisy's house, it was Daisy, her mom, dad, two sisters, two brothers, and one cat named Rocky.

"Stop shouting, Daisy!" I barked.

"I'm not shouting!" Daisy barked back.

She was so loud I couldn't hear myself think.

"Then be quiet."

Daisy smirked in a way that suggested she'd do no such thing. "What is *that*?"

Roaming the pond's edge was a three-foot-tall trespasser with skinny legs and a pointy beak.

"Go away," I roared at the big bird.

17

Daisy's mom, Marissa, called out, "Tali?"

Daisy loves Marissa and cries whenever she's away. I love Marissa, too, but I also love Daisy's dad, Bill, who taught me how to catch the ball-ball. The first time he threw the ball-ball to me, I wondered why it kept getting bigger and bigger and even bigger. Then it hit me, right between the eyes.

It didn't hurt.

Since then, I've always tried to catch the ball-ball, no matter how far or how high Bill throws it. I can't get enough of that ball or any ball, and that's why I call it ball-ball.

I swatted the air, attempting to chase away the big bird. In a gung ho tone, I barked, "GO AWAY!"

Marissa's frantic voice called out from the other side of the fence. "Binah, go get Mommy."

I barked louder. "Unless you're a stork here to deliver a puppy, fly away, you big feathered fowl!"

 Mommy opened the sliding glass door, stepped out onto the deck, and yelled, "DROP IT! DROP IT!" She ran past me toward the pond. The intruder dropped the fish, flew onto the shed next door, launched into the air like a helicopter, and flew out of sight.

"Tali, are you okay?" Marissa asked from behind the fence.

"Did you see the size of that thing?" Mommy bent down to the ground, cradled the fish, and gently placed it back into the water. "Was that an egret?" The fish floated there motionless. A ruckus was now going on among the other fish.

"I think so," Marissa said. "I've never seen a bird like that here. Do you want me to send Bill over?"

Bill? Yes, I thought. *Send Bill over. He can throw the ball-ball.*

"Would he mind taking the fish out? I can't do it."

I'm sorry, Mommy. I should've scared away the big bird.

Daisy wandered over toward Mommy and sat down on her foot. Mommy picked her up with one hand. Mommy needs two hands to pick me up because I'm a big girl.

Marissa answered, "I'm sorry, Tali. I'll send Bill over. Daisy, come home."

Mommy said, "She can stay. Binah would love Daisy to walk with us. I can bring her home afterward."

Daisy's little tongue kissed Mommy's cheek.

"Okay. Bill will take care of the fish before you get back."

"Thanks, Marissa." Mommy put Daisy down on the grass and said, "Girls, go pee," before waving us off. She disappeared behind the sliding glass door, leaving it open for us to follow.

I smelled a bunny. I ran around the bushes and sniffed underneath the shed.

Nothing.

I raced back to the pond where Daisy was busy sniffing the grass. "Hey, Daisy, why are fish so smart?"

Daisy thought for a few seconds, flashed her crowded teeth, and said, "Because they know moss code?"

"Morse code," I laughed. "That's pretty clever. Fish are smart because they stay in schools."

Her smile disappeared as she cocked her head, squinted her eyes, and asked, "Fish go to school?"

"Forget it," I said. "Come on, I'll race you to the door."

Inside, I heard Mommy moving around upstairs. I was certain that she was dividing my homemade meal into two bowls. Her footsteps got louder and louder until she appeared downstairs. "Who's hungry?"

Daisy said, "I am! I am!"

Mommy put down the bowls. "This one is for Daisy, and this one is for Binah."

I'm a good girl, I thought. *I wait patiently.*

Daisy danced around both bowls before tasting mine.

"Daisy," I whimpered.

Mommy said, "It's okay, Binah. You can have this one."

After finishing the first bowl, Daisy pranced around to the second bowl. That's when Mommy started the game "No."

"Daisy, no," Mommy said as she closed the back door.

Daisy was enjoying the second bowl of food.

"Daisy, NO!" Mommy said again.

It took all of six seconds for Daisy to polish off my bowl, which was initially her bowl.

I barked at Daisy, "My mommy said NO! What part don't you understand, the *N* or the *O*?"

Mommy said, "Binah, it's okay. I'll feed you upstairs."

Daisy was no longer allowed upstairs. More than once she had peed on the carpet. One time when we were upstairs, I went to my favorite place—my bed—circled three times, and sprawled out with a sigh. Daisy suddenly squatted and peed in the house.

In the house!

I barked, "Mommy!"

Daisy didn't dare look at me. With her tail between her legs, she weaved back and forth hastily and dropped her eyes again when Mommy came into the room. Mommy yelled, "No more peeing in the house, Daisy!"

After I ate my breakfast upstairs, we all went for a walk. Daisy and I found something deliciously dead to sniff, but our leashes pulled us away before we had time to roll in it.

I almost missed it, the impressive green creature sitting on a mound of dirt. It was a twig with legs and carried a green leaf on its back.

I'm telling you, it was spectacular.

"That's a praying mantis," Mommy said.

Daisy didn't see it at first. "What's a praying mantis?"

"Look," I said, pointing with my nose.

"Oh my God! Oh my GOD! OH MY GOD!" Daisy barked.

"Daisy, shush." Mommy lifted her up to quiet her down.

Mommy didn't shush me. I just watched Praying Mantis.

Mommy said, "Some people believe that praying mantises are the superheroes of bugs. Their special power is to transfer their courage to lost souls in order to guide them home."

Is this a sign? I wonder if Praying Mantis is leading Javi home.

21

Mommy said, "I bet Javi made friends with a praying mantis and followed his new friend over the Rainbow Bridge to the meadow where pets reunite with their loved ones after they die."

"I'll see you again, Praying Mantis," I whispered.

Mommy put Daisy back down onto the ground, and the three of us continued our walk to the park. There were three parks in the neighborhood, and we always went to the cleanest one, which we dogs called Starbarks Park.

Get it?

3
Javi

ONE DAY MY EYES OPENED, AND I COULD SEE THAT MAMA HAD short curly fur the color of caramelized sugar, just like me. I watched her belly rise and fall as she slept on her back. Princess Leia, sleeping on her belly with her eyes closed, rested her tiny head on Mama's side. My sister had mostly white fur with a few black specks splashed on her back. She lay very still. I moved away slowly, careful not to wake them, and rolled around on the floor that was as soft as Mama's fur.

In one part of the room, I played with my new friend, Allie Gator, whose soft body fit perfectly into my mouth. I loved her shades of blues and yellows as well as her squeak. In another part of the room, a framed photograph of my smiling humans hung on the wall. Neha, holding a bouquet of flowers, wore white lace over her long dark hair and had blushed cheeks and rose-colored lips.

Her fancy white dress flowed to the ground. Roger had jet-black curly hair and wore a white jacket with a black bow tie. They were both too happy to hide their teeth. Their eyes appeared to follow me as I roamed about the room. A photograph of little Oz sitting on Sarai's lap hung on a different wall. Their eyes didn't follow me. On a third wall was a photograph of Mama running on the grass. When I saw Mama and Princess Leia still sleeping on the doggy bed, I understood that these photographs were moments magically frozen in time.

Roger came into the room and said, "Good morning, Javi."

Good morning, Roger.

Dogs are more likely to be aware of smells than visuals. Unless we're really focused, we notice what humans smell like far more than what they look like or what they're wearing.

Roger didn't smell like his invigorated self. I wasn't sure but I thought I smelled fear. Because I was genuinely focused, I noticed that Roger's dark hair was messy. He was dressed in blue jeans and a crumpled white T-shirt. Short dark hairs grew on his jaw. Lines across his brow emerged. With one single hand, he lifted up my tiny sister.

He sharply called out, "Neha? Bring me a baby blanket."

Mama shifted her position and became restless.

Neha, still wearing her sleeping clothes, entered with a blanket. "What's the matter?"

Sarai, also in her sleeping clothes, walked in right behind her.

Roger said, "Princess Leia's gone. She must've passed during the night."

24

Neha moaned, "Oh no."

The smell of fear in the room intensified as Sarai began to cry.

Roger whispered, "It happens, Sarai. Sometimes a puppy is here for only a short time to teach us lessons that we can't learn without them. Princess Leia will now go home to heaven."

Sarai continued to cry. "Is she okay?"

"She'll be okay, Sarai," Neha whispered. "Princess Leia loved sharing your name."

"She knew?"

"Of course she knew that *Sarai* means 'princess.'"

"Does Javi know?"

I looked up at the sound of my name. I was happy to be distracted from not understanding what happened to my sister.

"Yes, Princess, Javi knows."

I wagged my tail lopsidedly clockwise, toward the right. I wag toward the left when I'm with someone unfamiliar, like a new human or dog.

"Does he know that I'm almost four years old?"

"Yes, Javi is very smart."

"Does he know that the name Oz means strong?"

"I'm not sure." Neha's forehead wrinkled in pretend confusion. "Would you like to tell him?"

"Javi, do you know that my baby brother is strong?"

I heard Sarai, but I was more focused on this thing outside the window. It was mainly green and looked like a twig with legs. It was big, twice the size of my paw. I jumped up from the couch onto the window shelf to get a closer look.

I barked, "What in the world is that creepy crawler?"

Sarai caught on. "Daddy, look. It's a praying auntie."

"It's pronounced praying *mantis*," Roger said. "Some people believe they have supernatural powers."

Sarai said, "What does that mean?"

"They're like superheroes who show lost travelers the way home to heaven."

"Do you think he's here to show Princess Leia the way home?"

Roger smiled and hugged Sarai. "That's what I was just thinking, baby girl."

I howled out the window. "Awoooooooooooooooooooo."

Please take my baby sister home to heaven, I thought.

Praying Mantis didn't answer me.

4
Binah

WOW! IF JAVI CAN BELIEVE THAT PRAYING MANTIS CAN TAKE Princess Leia home, then I can believe that Praying Mantis can take Javi home.

Right?

So after we saw Praying Mantis, Mommy, Daisy, and I walked to Starbarks Park. It had endless grass to tumble over and just the right amount of dirt to stain our fur. On rainy days the scattered puddles lasted for days.

Big trees with lots of leaves surrounded the park's metal fence. When the weather got cold, and the leaves fell off the trees, we loved sniffing them and jumping into the leaf piles as they crunched beneath our paws. We especially loved rolling around in them after the rain when the leaves began to rot.

Yup, Starbarks was our favorite gigantic backyard.

Daisy and I met up with Chloe, our other best friend.

"Hi, Bean." Chloe ran over, sniffed me, and got a whiff of all the dogs and humans I had met since I saw her last.

"Hi, Chloe," I said as I circled her and her long beautiful hair.

"Hi, Daisy."

"Hey, Chloe."

Mommy freed us from our leashes, threw the ball-ball for me, and sat down next to Chloe's mom, Phyllis.

I love Phyllis. She always spoke to me in a cheerful voice, gently petted me, and, most importantly, kept yummy treats in her pocket. She rewarded me with a treat whenever I gave her a high-five. Sometimes I got a treat simply because Chloe got one.

We all ran around. Some of us fetched balls—me. Some of us rolled around in the dirt or mud—Daisy. And some of us tossed our hair—Chloe. We varied in size. Daisy was eight pounds soaking wet. She was short and slender with a little nose, little legs, long ears, a stub for a tail, and crooked bottom teeth. She hated her teeth, but I thought it was a cute character trait that belonged only to her.

Chloe was about thirty pounds. She was tall with long legs, long ears, curious eyes, and a long snout. Her white feathered tail looked like mine, except for where she habitually bit it. The rest of her body hair was, as I already mentioned, long and beautiful. I haven't weighed eight pounds since I was a puppy and if I ever weigh thirty pounds, Mommy will need three hands to pick me up.

It's our differences rather than our similarities that make us best friends.

It was Chloe who spotted the new dog. Not new like a puppy, but new like we never saw him before. He swatted at the air like he was dodging an airplane.

Definitely cuckoo for Cocoa Puffs. How do I know this reference? Television commercials.

"I'm Chloe," Chloe said. "And they are Binah and Daisy."

Now standing still, I saw remnants of a spider's web dangling from his face. He was a handsome black and white cockapoo who had a sock hanging from his mouth. "I'm Cooper," he said. "Binah's a pretty name."

I looked at his pink lips and half-pink and half-black nose and said, "It means understanding."

His eyes were brown.

"What means understanding?" Cooper asked.

"My name means understanding."

No wait, half of one eye was blue.

"My name means understanding?" Cooper said, confused.

"I don't know what your name means. My name, Binah, means understanding."

"Pretty name."

Daisy said, "Cooper, my dad collects cars. Are you named after the car, Mini Cooper?"

"I don't know," Cooper replied as he sniffed all eight pounds of Daisy.

Daisy smiled, displaying her little crooked teeth, and said, "Do you know the neighborhood dogs, Mercedes, Bentley, and Royce?"

"Royce?" Cooper asked mystified.

"As in Rolls, baby!" I laughed.

Cooper answered. "The names sound familiar. I know Bentley lives around the corner from me."

Chloe rejoined the conversation. "We're all neighbors."

Cooper gave Chloe a once-over. "Who are you again?"

"Chloe," said Chloe. She bit her tail and shook her long locks as if she just got out of the bath.

"Porsche and Lexus too. They're all named after cars." Daisy said flirtatiously.

"Named after cars?" Cooper tilted his head.

I interrupted their unlikely romance. "Hey, Daisy, why are there so many cars named after animals, but none named after dogs?"

Daisy circled Cooper and said, "Interesting question, Binah."

"Cars named after animals?" Cooper tilted his head again.

As if she were naming her favorite snacks, Daisy said, "There's the jaguar, cougar, and the rabbit."

You go, girl!

I said, "Whaddaya call a bunch of rabbits walking backward?"

Daisy ignored my riddle. "The mustang, tiger, and stingray."

Poor Daisy was wasting her charm on a boy who was clueless.

"A receding *hare* line." I laughed at my own punch line.

Daisy continued, "Also the bronco, impala, and bluebird."

Now she was just showing off.

I sang out, "And, the bar-ra-coo-da."

Daisy declared, "The Chrysler Eagle should be changed to the Chrysler Beagle."

"Very clever, Daisy," Chloe said.

"And Mitsubishi to Mitsushihtzu after Javi."

"Aw, thank you, Daze," I said. "That's very sweet."

"And Datsun to Dachshund."

Daisy really is very clever.

"Nissan to Bichon," I said thinking about Mommy's car.

Cooper's mommy called for him. "Cheerio," he said.

"Fruit Loop," I called out.

"Fruit Loop," Daisy and Chloe said in surround sound.

Only Starbarks Park can change strangers into friends. And only God knows why, the four of us stayed best friends forever.

5
Javi

My FIRST FEW MONTHS WERE CRITICAL LEARNING PERIODS. The more I practiced the commands from my humans, the easier it got and the faster I learned. Although I quickly learned to understand Roger's tone of voice, it took me longer to learn the meaning of some words he used. For example, "good boy" almost always produced a yummy treat to eat, but the word *no* was confusing. At first, I thought it meant "try again." But sometimes when I tried again, I got a second no and a tap on my nose. I hated the tap on my nose. So then I thought *no* meant "stop," but sometimes when I stopped, I'd hear, "try again." When I tried again, I'd hear "good boy" and get a treat.

See what I mean?

I discussed this with Mama who confirmed my thoughts. "Humans can be complicated."

One morning, when we were all eating breakfast, Neha said to Sarai, "Did you know that Javi's sense of taste is stronger than his hearing, and his sense of smell is more powerful than his sight?"

That's true. I sniff to see, not smell. I see through my nose.

"What do I do better, Mommy?" asked Sarai.

"You can see better than you can hear, and you can smell better than you can taste."

"That's a miracle, Mommy."

"You're a miracle, Princess."

"How am I a miracle?"

"You're a miracle because, although you came *through* me, you come *from* God."

"Is Oz a miracle?"

"Yes," Neha said as she fed Oz with one hand and patted me with the other. "We all are."

Almost every morning, Roger, Mama, and I walked Sarai to the school bus. The three of us waited with the big humans until Sarai and the other little humans climbed inside the bus. Seconds later, Sarai's little face appeared pressed against the window as her thumb and four fingers waved goodbye to us.

"That's my girl," Roger said and smiled as he waved back.

"That's my girl," Mama barked.

33

"That's my girl!" I echoed as I stood up on my hind legs. All the big humans waved goodbye and said, "Have a great day!" and "I love you!"

I love big humans.

Back home, Mama taught me the importance of listening. "Listen to everyone," she said.

"What if they're boring?"

"Listen anyway."

"What if I disagree with them?"

"Then definitely listen. You never know who carries a special message for you."

Mama and I listened to Neha sing the alphabet to Oz over and over again: "Now I know my ABC's. Next time won't you sing with me?"

Neha also sang a song about Jonah and the whale.

"Who did, who did, who did, who did, who did swallow Jo- Jo- Jonah?"

I loved the singing.

"Whale did, whale did, whale did, whale did, whale did swallow Jo- Jo- Jonah."

I said to Mama, "Mama, I find this story hard to believe. How could Jonah live in the whale's belly?"

"It's a miracle," Mama said. "Like Jonah, we each have a mission. If we ignore it, we can end up lost in a dark place. This darkness hopefully causes us to search for light and puts us back on track."

I wonder what my mission is.

After my short afternoon nap, Neha wrapped Oz in a blanket and put him in the stroller while Mama and I walked with them to get Sarai. As soon as she stepped off the bus, I danced all around her and sniffed things that touched her throughout the day.

I smell cheese, grass, and apple juice.

Once home, Mama and Oz took a nap. I sat with Sarai and listened to Neha read from our favorite story book. We loved the story about an old man named Geppetto who made things out of wood. Geppetto was lonely because his wife went over the Rainbow Bridge, and he didn't have any little humans to love. One day he carved out a boy marionette and named him Pinocchio. This marionette changed into a real-life little boy, and together they had many adventures.

After dinner, I had my own adventure in the backyard. I learned about dandelions.

Roger told Sarai that it's the only flower that represents the sun, the moon, and the stars. He said, "The yellow flower implies the sun, the puff ball resembles the moon, and when you blow it, its seeds look like tiny stars." He pulled out a single dandelion puff, held it out to Sarai, and said, "These magical flowers just might help make your dreams come true."

"Really?" Sarai was excited as she cradled the flower.

Roger said, "Close your eyes, make a wish, and blow, blow, blow like the wind."

I watched Sarai close her eyes.

I closed my eyes, too.

I thought about what I ultimately wanted. More than anything, I wanted to transform into a real-life little boy just like Pinocchio did, and to make friends with my creator. When I made my wish, something stirred deep within my heart and soul.

After we blew, blew, blew like the wind, we chased after the scattering seeds as if they really were stars.

6
Javi

"Mama?"

"Yes, Javi?"

"Whatever happened to my brother?"

"You don't have a brother. You had a sister. I gave birth to only two pups."

"But, Mama, my brother spoke to me. Although I didn't see him, I heard him. He told me to be afraid."

Mama whispered, "That must've been your inner voice."

"What inner voice?"

"It's time for me to share a story with you that my mama shared with me a long time ago."

I was excited. I loved listening to stories.

"All puppies are born with genes that are passed down from their mama and papa. Each gene carries specific information that makes up who the puppy will be. Sometimes a gene is activated right away, like the fibroblast growth factor 5 gene."

I cocked my head, first toward the right and then toward the left.

Mama said, "This FGF5 gene determines if the puppy's coat will be long or short. Other times a gene is not activated right away, like the melon collie gene. Your inner negative voice saying, '*be afraid,*' is one way to wake up melon collie. The fear causes chemicals to be released from the body. The end result is feelings of sadness."

"There's more than one way to wake up melon collie?"

"Yes, Javi. The second way is to allow external voices to activate it. This is most likely triggered by a human's negative words or actions."

I was still confused. "How can a human activate a dog's gene?"

"Melon collie can be activated when dogs are physically or verbally abused by humans."

I roared, "WHAT! Why would a human do that?"

"I don't have the answer. Perhaps they were abused themselves, and they don't fully understand that repeating the behavior, even to a dog, can leave visible and invisible scars."

"Mama, that's so sad."

"Exactly! See, just talking about it stirs melon collie. Also, not giving dogs the attention they need may create an inner negative voice. '*Nobody cares about me*' or '*I'm unlovable.*'"

"I understand, Mama. So, what happens once melon collie is activated?"

"Once melon collie is activated, the brain sends a signal to the body to release chemicals into the bloodstream. These chemicals travel back to the brain and cause the puppy to be sad."

"Oooh. And these chemicals smells, right?"

"Yes, Javi. Dogs can smell melon collie."

"Can we smell melon collie in humans?"

"In humans we can easily detect their release of something called stress hormones."

"Mama, is this preventable?"

"Yes and no. Prior to melon collie being activated, he'll knock on the door of your mind. You don't have to answer him. If you choose to open the door, melon collie will definitely come in, make a mess of your thoughts, and try to steal your happiness."

I wanted to confirm that I understood what Mama was saying. "So, if someone says something negative about me, I don't have to internalize it?"

"That's correct, Javi, but it's not easy. We can't control the negative behaviors of others. We can only control how we perceive their behaviors by choosing not to take their hurtful words or actions personally. This is definitely easier for a dog with an old soul because they've had the most practice. Dogs with infant souls have the least amount of experience and will struggle the most because they believe every action needs a reaction. Infant souls convince themselves that their behaviors are a result of something that happened, something somebody said or did to them."

"Am I an infant soul, Mama?"

"Javi, I think you're an old soul, but at times, when you focus on what you *don't* have, which can make you feel sad, rather than focus on what you *do* have, which can make you feel happy, then yes, your infant soul will express itself. We all have two voices in our head. One is a loud negative voice, and the other is a soft positive whisper. Every day, you get to choose which voice wins your attention."

Mama did the best she could to prepare me for the future. "You'll travel many roads while discovering your life's purpose. It's inevitable that you'll hear the negative voices and experience melon collie along the way."

"Can I avoid melon collie?"

"Yes and no. Melon collie may knock often on the door. You can choose to ignore it. You're more likely to open the door when you're vulnerable. Be strong. Try not to open the door."

"Let's say I'm vulnerable, and I open the door, Mama. How do I get rid of melon collie?"

"If you invite melon collie in, keep the visit short. You'll feel uncomfortable, which isn't a bad thing. Feeling uncomfortable gives you an opportunity to change for the better." Mama kissed me. "Look for the lessons and then kick the negative voices and melon collie out as fast as you can."

"Okay, Mama."

"Now, say goodbye."

"Say goodbye?"

Mama kissed me again. "Say goodbye."

"Where're we going?"

"You're moving to a new home with Roger and his family, and I'm going to stay with another family because Roger doesn't have room for me."

"I'm going to miss you, Mama."

"I'm going to miss you more. But, it's okay. One day you'll understand that our homes are only temporary."

I heard my brother's voice—I mean, *my* negative voice—inside my head.

Be afraid.

I whimpered. "Mama. Please don't go."

"Sometimes, we have to do things we don't want to do. Never look back. Remember that miracles don't happen when we feel our best. They happen when we feel uncomfortable. Don't let the negative voices talk you out of your destiny."

I looked at Mama lovingly and asked, "What did the puppy say to his mama after breast feeding?"

"Tell me, my prince."

"Thanks for the mammaries."

I can still hear the echo of Mama's laughter.

7

Binah

EVEN THOUGH I DON'T QUITE UNDERSTAND IT, I CAN TELL THAT the negative voices and melon collie are important. Javi was lucky to have spent some time with his mama. It seems like he learned a lot from her, and I'm learning a lot, too. I now know when the seed of becoming a little boy was planted in Javi's brain. I wish I could've experienced the story of Pinocchio with Javi. I bet he would've paused the book or the movie several times to discuss what life lessons he had learned from his humans.

Chloe was already at Starbarks Park stalking Cooper, who had just completed the play slap, the loud stomping of his two forefeet at once. Before that, he had unsuccessfully asked some unknown dog to play with him.

Me: "Making friends again, Cooper?"

Cooper: "Hi, Understanding."

I sighed loudly. "My name is Binah. *Beeee-naaaa*." I dragged out the word as though Cooper didn't understand English. "What's with the sock?"

Cooper: "It's my thing."

Chloe scratched her tail and said, "Hi, Cooper."

Cooper: "Hi. Where's the other one?"

Me: "Daisy?"

Cooper: "Who runs in circles creating swirly dust?"

Me: "That would be Daisy. She's home."

Cooper: "Today's my birthday. I'm two years old."

Chloe bit her tail and said, "I'm one, but I like older dogs."

Me: "Happy birthday, Cooper."

Cooper: "I had two servings of birthday cake. It's no surprise that I'm five pounds overweight."

Chloe: "I'm average weight, but I like big dogs."

Cooper: "I'm obsessed with food."

Me: "I thought you were obsessed with socks?"

Cooper: "I never said that."

Me: "You always have one hanging out of your mouth."

Cooper: "That's because I love socks. They're cool."

Me: "Trust me, they're not cool. They're the opposite of cool."

Chloe: "I love peanut butter. I could eat it every day."

Cooper: "I don't like peanut butter."

Chloe: "Me neither."

Me: "I love peanut butter."

Cooper: "I guess I should learn to love peanut butter to fit in.

You know, go with the flow."

Me: "You don't have to love peanut butter to be our friend, Cooper. My brother, Javi, taught me that our inner negative voice makes us vulnerable to *go* with the flow while our inner positive voice empowers us to *be* the flow.

Cooper: "What?"

Me: "Our inner negative voice tempts us to say and do things that activate melon collie and make us feel sad."

Before prancing off, Cooper called me crazy.

Nobody likes to be called bad names, not even a dog.

This suddenly triggered my inner negative voice. When I got home, I tore Mommy's newspaper into pieces and then spit it out like confetti.

Mommy walked into the room. She was not happy. "Binah, did you make this mess?"

I went to her with my head down, my ears back and my tail between my legs.

No.

"Who made this mess?"

I don't know.

"Binah?"

Ashamed, I knelt down and covered my eyes with my paws. There's a stranger in my head. Someone I can't see or smell, but whom I can only hear. That stranger is my inner negative voice.

I whimpered, "I'm sorry, Mommy. I made this mess. I'm not feeling my best."

Mommy knew that I missed Javi. We both did.

8
Javi

SOMETIME LATER, THE HUMANS MOVED INTO THEIR NEW HOME. Six-year-old Sarai, four-year-old Oz, and I (now two years old) stayed with Aunt Liz, Uncle Ron, and Cousin Susie.

I thought my eyes were deceiving me. Uncle Ron and Roger looked nearly identical. Both of them were forty-something, had black beards speckled with gray in some places and dark brown eyes. They were about the same height, as tall as the refrigerator, and even walked the same.

Thank goodness for my nose. They didn't smell the same. Roger smelled like citrus and the woody outdoors. Ron smelled mostly like cigarette smoke. I don't like the smell of smoke.

I heard that Susie was a few years older than Sarai, and Elvis was their brand new five-year-old puppy. I didn't understand how a puppy can be five years old.

45

"Susie," Aunt Liz called out. "Go downstairs. Give the dogs a treat, and put fresh water in the bowl."

"Okay, Mom," Susie called back.

I smelled him before I heard him, and I heard him before I saw him. Holy cow, he was enormous. The blotches of brown fur on his chest were bigger than I was. Understand, he wasn't just enormous compared to me. He was enormous compared to every other dog I'd ever seen. He was bigger than Sarai and Susie combined. He had a lean body, a head the size of a basketball, and a tongue the size of my face. Aside from the boo-boo bandage on his tail, he looked like a horse.

Susie held food out to Sarai. "Do you want to feed Elvis?"

"Okay." Sarai giggled as she took the golf ball-size treats.

He shoved his gigantic head under Sarai's hand. His eyes widened when he saw me.

Oh God! I thought. *Please finish your treat.*

He circled me.

My tail twitched nervously toward the left. I imagined Elvis debating: treat or fourteen pounds of fresh meat?

After sniffing my submissive body, he kissed me with his tongue that was as big as my face. He liked me. Elvis ran around the room like the horse I thought he was. I couldn't believe he didn't break anything. His ears dropped a little, and his boo-boo bandaged tail wagged a lot. He licked me again. The Great Dane really liked me.

After he bowed, using the old high-rump approach, he invited me to rumble. His message was clear: he intended to play with me, not eat me. He dropped to the ground to handicap himself. This evened out the playing field. When his thirty-four-inch, one hundred seventy pound body (I heard these numbers from Uncle Ron) accidentally hit me too hard, I scurried backward.

He apologized with a gentle play slap with his paw. "I'm sorry, little guy."

Okay, ya big palooka.

Right when I rushed directly back into his face, the basement door opened. A beautiful, skinny poodle with black curly fur and beautiful green eyes that sparkled like emeralds traipsed down like a ballerina.

Elvis barked excitedly, "Hi, Misty."

Susie was excited, too. "Hi, Misty. I want you to meet my cousin Sarai and her brother, Javi."

Sarai called out, "Hi, Misty."

"Hello," Misty softly barked. "I live next door."

Elvis barked, "Javi just moved into the neighborhood."

"Welcome," Misty whispered as she moved to the blue bowl, home to the normal-size dry kibble. She quickly ate every last morsel and sighed. "Is there more food?"

Susie caught on. "Are you hungry, Misty?"

Two barks: "Yes. Yes, I am."

Susie opened a cabinet and took out a bag of treats. I could smell that they were stale, but I still wanted one.

Misty yapped, "My busy family forgets to feed me so I learned to hide some of my food, but I'm always hungry."

I'm trained to eat twice a day, I thought. *I'm hardly ever hungry.*

What I actually said was, "That's very smart, Misty."

"Sometimes I lose control, and I eat until I throw up. My humans get mad and take away my food." Misty sounded sad.

I'd bet that her melon collie gene had been activated. Her brain had already sent a signal to her body to release chemicals into her bloodstream.

"It's common to lose control, Misty," I said wanting to sound supportive. "Sometimes, when we take more than we need, we end up with nothing."

Elvis barked, "We all struggle with something, Misty. I bite my tail until it bleeds." His big ears were now pulled back and pressed down against his head. His tail with its boo-boo was tucked between his legs. "My new dad, Ron, said my first dad, Greg, was an angry human who drank too much alcohol." Elvis looked away as his body slumped into a submissive posture.

"I'm sorry, Elvis," I said. "Hurt humans hurt others. How did you get your second family?"

"Ron worked with Greg. One night, Greg didn't come home. He didn't come home the next night either. Ron came by the house and took me out of my dirty crate. I was so ashamed. Ron washed me, fed me, and brought me here. I never went back."

"What happened to Greg?" I asked.

Misty cut in on the conversation. "My dad said Greg was locked in a human crate because his car was drunk and hit another car, or something like that."

"I love it here," Elvis said. "My new family never yells at me. They love me, and I'll always protect them."

"Elvis, you're a gentle giant with a big heart," I barked softly. "I'm curious, though, about why you still bite your tail."

Elvis said, "I guess for me it's a habit. I find it really hard to stop because I've been doing it since I was a puppy, and I'm now five years old. G.I. Joe helps me. He's been with me from the start."

Misty, who had been eating the entire time, stopped chewing. "You never mentioned G.I. Joe before."

Elvis said, "G.I. Joe is my superhero. He silently reminds me to not bite my tail. He's the only thing I have from my puppyhood." He galloped over to his bed, picked up a small plastic toy, and put it down at Misty's paws.

Misty first sniffed and then licked the green toy. "Hi, G.I. Joe. Where's your cape?"

"Not all superheroes wear capes," I said as I blinked at Misty.

Elvis interrupted. "Actually, Ron gave G.I. Joe an invisible superhero cape. He told me it would miraculously protect me and it would never come off unless I took it off."

Sometimes, believing in miracles makes living more bearable.

Susie opened the back door, and the three of us raced around outside in the plush grass while our little humans collected whimsical flowers.

"So many weeds," Susie said as she grabbed them by the handful.

"Dandelions aren't weeds," Sarai said. "They're magical flowers." She closed her eyes, paused for several seconds, pursed her lips, and blew. The white fluffy matter whooshed apart and floated in the direction of the wind. "My dad told me that dandelion wishes come true."

With my mouth, I pulled up one of the many magical flowers still planted in the grass. Imitating Sarai, I closed my eyes and made a wish. It was always the same one.

I wish to come back as a little boy.

And then I blew, blew, blew the seeds into the gentle wind.

That night I shared the bed with Elvis. In my sleep, my paws moved like they were galloping through the pasture. I awoke to my muffled, jowl-puffing barks. I twitched as I recalled Jiminy Cricket singing the song from the movie *Pinocchio,* "When You Wish upon a Star."

9
Binah

"Not all superheroes wear capes."

I love it!

Daisy shrieked when I play-bit her. I stopped in shock, "What'd I do?"

Drama queen, I thought.

She replied with a puzzled look. "Is that lickable?"

"Is what lickable?" I lay down, my head between my paws.

Daisy's chin pointed toward the UMO, unidentified moving object.

"Everything's lickable," I said with gusto because UMOs are especially thrilling to explore. Because it was my house, Daisy knew I had first dibs to sniff, lick, eat, sit on, or roll in anything. I grew curious as the UMO moved a short stretch away. My nose worked to identify it as my mouth studied it further by having my tongue perform taste tests.

Daisy interrupted. "Okay, Scooby-Doo, what is it?"

"I think it's a cricket," I said.

"Can I taste it?"

"You can have it."

Mommy came downstairs with our home-cooked chicken, rice, and carrots. We polished all of it off in six seconds and then met Chloe before heading over to Starbarks Park.

During our walk I noticed that humans need their space, about eighteen inches of space when standing. I've actually seen humans walk together and talk to one another from across the street. That's a lot of space. Do you know how much space dogs prefer? Zero.

Even though Tali walked Daisy and me, and Phyllis walked Chloe close enough together, we strove to shrink the space even more. We'd run in circles until our leashes blended into one.

At the park, the same sock dangled from the same mouth.

Cooper: "Well, if it isn't the Fruit Loop Brigade."

Daisy: "Hi, Cooper."

Daisy danced the hokey pokey on one side of him while I stood on the other side. We were positioned liked bookends, two pairs of naughty eyes.

Me: "Daisy, what did the left eye say to the right eye?"

Daisy: "Um, I don't know. What?"

Me: "Between you and me, something smells."

Daisy thought long and hard before laughing nervously. "Oh, I get it. The nose smells. That's clever, right?" She cocked her head before whispering, "Is this a joke?"

Me: "Not yet, but now look at who's between you and me."

Daisy: "Oh, that's hysterical. Between you and me is Cooper, so Cooper smells."

Cooper: "Hardy har har."

Me: "So when are you gonna say goodbye to that sock?"

Cooper: "Next time we meet."

Me: "You say that to feel better about not doing it now. Just drop the sock. You don't have to knock it outta the park."

Cooper: "No, really, I'll try next time."

Me: "Saying you'll try doesn't change anything. There's trying, and there's doing."

Cooper: "How about this: I'll try until I'm really tired, and then I'll do it."

Me: "What kind of dog do you want to be? The dog who's thinking about doing it, the dog who's talking about doing it, or the dog who's actually doing it?"

Cooper didn't answer me. With his sock dangling from his mouth, he ran around the bushes. He stopped to mark every other one. Chloe was biting her tail. Daisy scratched her back in the dirt, exposing her belly and making her more submissive than usual. Cooper yawned. Perhaps he was anxious. He wasn't ready to change. Or maybe it was a sign that a puppy somewhere had transformed into a human. I learned this song from Javi:

"Sometimes when a puppy yawns,

an angel dog will transform

into a human spirit just reborn.

La-la-la-la-la-de-da."

10
Javi

A FEW MONTHS AFTER WE SETTLED INTO THE HOUSE, NEHA GOT a new tree to live inside the house with us.

Inside.

I sniffed it in search of another dog scent.

Nothing.

I lifted my leg, happy to be the first one to mark the spot.

Neha cried out, "Java, NO!"

The second I heard Ja*va* instead of Ja*vi*, I knew I was in trouble.

"Outside. Now. GET OUT!"

In the fresh air, I explored the backyard, taste-tested the fresh insects, pooped on the grass, and then rolled around on it. Roger came out twice: once to hose me down—this is a very disturbing game—and again to feed me. It was getting dark, and I was ready to go back inside.

"Stay!" Roger said, as he closed the door.

A few years later, Inside Tree would betray me a second time after Sarai dressed as Princess and Oz dressed as Superboy. We had walked the neighborhood collecting "treats."

Everybody knows you can't show treats to a dog, leave them out in a challenging, but not death-defying location, go to bed, and expect there to be an uneventful night. Right?

It was dark. Everyone, including me, was asleep. It was my inner negative voice who woke me up.

"Come here, Javi," he said.

"I'm sleeping."

"You're not sleeping. Come here."

I left my comfortable bed in the living room. "Where are you?"

I knew exactly where he was.

"I'm in the den."

"We're not allowed in the den."

"We're not allowed in the den," he mimicked me.

I hate it when he does that.

"Come smell all these treats," he said tormenting me.

I passed through the half-open door. The room was pitch black except for the pale-blue light that crept through from the bathroom night-light. There was just enough light for me to make out my surroundings and the treats that lay before me. The sky above the ceiling window was black with a few specks of stars. I inhaled the powerful bouquet of pleasures.

"Let's go, Javi. You know you want to."

"I don't want to get into trouble."

"Trouble, schmuble. Everyone's asleep. Nobody'll know."

I heard Mama's voice. "Your inner negative voice can activate melon collie and make you more vulnerable to become a follower and *go* with the flow. Use your positive inner voice to empower you to become a leader and *be* the flow."

The next thing I knew, a bag of treats spilled over onto the floor. I ripped into every wrapper. I taste-tested something dark wrapped in something shiny. It was shaped like a teardrop and tasted yummy. I ate some more and then decided to hide some for the next day.

I spotted Inside Tree.

It was my inner voice who said, "Gee, I'm smart, ain't I?"

I buried my treasure deep in the dirt, pawed the earth back over it and patted the dirt when I was done so it would look untouched. I licked my paws clean to hide the evidence, shook myself off and took a deep breath so I would look innocent. Then I felt dizzy. I thought it was all the excitement, but then I felt nauseous.

BLAUGGGGHHHH.

I pooped, and then I vomited—again and again and again. My inner negative voice activated melon collie. My brain sent a signal to my body to release chemicals into my bloodstream causing me to be sad.

I should've listened to Mama.

11
Binah

Daisy: "TELL ME AGAIN WHO MELON COLLIE IS."

Cooper: "According to Professor Binah, *our* negative thoughts can become our negative voice and make us say and do negative things. This activates melon collie and causes us to be sad."

How do you like that? Cooper was listening.

Me: "Impressive, Cooper. I just want to add one important thing. We can learn to change our negative thoughts into positive ones and prevent activating melon collie."

Daisy: "How do we do that?"

Me: "We practice. We learn from our mistakes by trying not to repeat them." I looked at Chloe and said, "Like biting your tail." Then, I looked at Daisy and said, "And peeing in the house."

Daisy's eyes widened, raising the ridge above her eyes.

If looks could kill.

Me: "You're good girls, and you're smart enough to know that you're never too old to change."

Cooper: "What about me, Binah?"

Me: "Cooper, you're a mover and a shaker."

Cooper: "You hear that, girls? I'm a mover and a shaker."

Me: "But from a place of insecurity."

Cooper: "What? Girls, don't listen to her."

Me: "You chase after things you believe will bring instant joy without ever stopping to think about why."

Cooper: "Like what?"

Me: "Like socks and attention. Whatever it is, you want it right now."

Cooper: "That's absurd." He picked up his sock and ran off.

Daisy: "Binah, what do you struggle to change?"

Me: "Ever since Javi went over the Rainbow Bridge, I struggle with melon collie. But I'm working on it. Javi told me that it would get easier. He's my hero."

He'll always be my hero.

12
Javi

EVERYTHING SMELLED STERILE WHEN I RETURNED HOME FROM the hospital. I walked into Sarai's bedroom, my new safe haven. Lots of stuffed animals, much bigger than Allie Gator, slept on Sarai's bed. I lay down on the soft rug. A few inches away Raggedy Ann and Andy shared a rocking chair. Next to them was a tipped-over box of colorful plastic building blocks. I was startled by another dog resting nearby. She was beautiful. Why didn't anyone tell me that I had a new playmate?

"Hi," we both barked at the same time.

I smiled.

She smiled.

I got up, walked closer, and bowed down.

She did the same thing at the same time.

I stood up on my back paws.

So did she.

Ooh, okay. I noticed she was a he.

I moved closer and made a face.

He made the same face.

This was fun.

I blew bubbles with my spit and showed him my tongue.

He blew bubbles with his spit and showed me his tongue.

Wow. He had a heart-shaped birthmark, too.

Sarai walked in.

"Hi, Sarai," we both barked.

"Hey, Javi, meet Javi."

I was confused.

The moment Sarai picked me up, and I saw that she was holding the other dog, I discovered me.

Sarai said, "Mommy said it's time for you to go outside."

Out on the patio, where the rainwater pooled, my inner negative voice said to me, "Whaddaya see when you look in the puddle?"

I knew this was a dangerous question and had the potential to activate melon collie.

I said, "I don't see me as I am."

"Whaddaya mean, 'me as I am'?" asked my inner voice.

"I don't see a dog. I see a boy, a real-life, little boy!"

My inner negative voice laughed and barked, "You're deeply disturbed."

I barked back, "Don't laugh at me. Don't call me names. Mama taught me that I can become whatever I want."

My negative voice barked back louder. "You and your dreams, your hopefulness, and your optimism. You're a dog! You were a dog yesterday, you're a dog today, and you'll be a dog tomorrow."

I fought hard to hear Mama's voice. It was only a whisper, but she reminded me to never give up on my dream.

I wish one day to wake up as a little boy I thought.

I woke up the next morning.

Wish denied.

I felt love for everyone but my inner negative voice.

One night, while I was out on a walk with Roger, I bumped into Misty walking with her dad. Staring into her deep green eyes, I wondered if under her lids she dreamed about me when she slept.

"Hi, handsome."

"Misty!" My tail wagged clockwise until a loud bark scared me.

"Don't worry," Misty said. "That old dog is harmless."

Sniffing the grass, I found fresh pee mail that read "I'm the greatest."

"Hey, Misty, do you know this signature?"

Sniff. Sniff.

"That's Ali. He's the loud barker. He thinks he's a two-year-old boxer, but he's really a thirteen-year-old bulldog. Don't let his loud bark scare you." And then, for the first time, Misty kissed me. I felt a jolt of electricity race through my body.

Do dogs get goose bumps? You bet we do.

Goose bumpy skin appeared beneath my fur just as the front door of a house opened. I panicked as the little dog raced down the steps toward us. My tail involuntarily twitched toward the left.

Misty barked, "Ali won't test you for what you can take. He'll test you for what you won't take. Stand up for yourself, Javi."

I looked at Ali's pug-like face. His bold and confident bowling ball eyes were intense, and his thinning ebony fur was tucked behind his pink ears. His body trembled as he barked loud and fast. "If you're gonna fight, fight. If you're gonna kiss, get a room."

"WE'RE NOT FIGHTING," Misty yelled. "JAVI'S NEW IN TOWN!"

I whispered, "Misty, why are you screaming?"

She whispered back, "Because Ali's deaf."

Ali created a ruckus. "I'm the greatest boxer in the world." He sniffed me and rubbed his fur against mine.

I licked him to let him know that I wasn't a threat.

Ali sniffed me again, squatted to pee and said in a gravelly voice, "What are you, a shih tzu?"

"Yes," I said as I licked him again.

Being licked by a dog can cheer up anybody, even another dog.

Ali said with enough spit to egg on a fight, "You should be an envelope. That's the only way you'll ever get licked."

I backed away. I learned that dogs showed who they really were. I used to ignore it because I wanted them to be who I wanted them to be.

Ali tried to break the frosty atmosphere. In a softer voice, thumping his tail against the ground with every sentence, he said,

"Hey, I don't mean any harm."

Thump.

"I'm no boxer."

Thump.

"I'm a bulldog."

Thump.

"If you were a girl shih tzu, and we had pups, we'd create a breed of bullshiht."

Thump.

He chuckled.

When Misty laughed, I relaxed and giggled, too. The old dog was funny.

13

Javi

It was November 23, 2005, my sixth birthday. At six years old, I was still trying to rise above my negative voice and avoid melon collie. I wanted so much to learn from my mistakes.

After dinner everyone, except for Neha, went into the balloon-decorated living room. Oz played with his collection of toy cars, racing them from one end of the room to another. Roger sat down on the couch while Sarai sat down on the piano bench. Her long delicate fingers touched the ebony and ivory keys and made music. Neha soon walked into the room carrying a plate with a glowing candle on top of my little doggy cake.

Everyone sang, "Happy birthday to Javi." Sarai and Oz chanted for me to make a wish. My wish never ever changed.

I want to be a little boy.

As the kids blew out my candle, I couldn't help but wonder what was most likely to come true: birthday wishes, dandelion wishes, or bedtime prayers?

Neha put my plate, with small pieces of cake on it, onto the floor. She served the kids their cake and sat down on the opposite end of the couch from Roger. She slowly positioned herself, putting her feet up onto Roger's lap. Roger intuitively knew to massage her feet. Neha's miracle-making hormones caused both her feet and her belly to swell.

I understood that they were having a baby. I was in the room when Neha and Roger shared the news with Sarai and Oz. Ten-year-old Sarai hoped for a sister, and eight-year-old Oz prayed for a brother. Like Sarai, I, too, wished for a baby sister. I missed Princess Leia. We would've been celebrating her birthday too.

Neha called out, "It's time for presents."

There's no time like the present to present the presents.

"I go first," Oz said as he slowly uncurled his fingers in front of me. "Javi, this is Silver Car. It's from my Matchbox collection."

I love Silver Car. Is this really for me?

"My turn." Sarai squatted down in front of me. "This is Blue Sweater," she said as she dressed me like her Raggedy Andy doll.

NOTE TO ALL HUMANS: Although I love Blue Sweater, my one coat is enough. Covering my back, chest, and sometimes my head makes me feel like I'm being squeezed into iron-clad armor that even Superdog can't escape from. Understand?

Sarai said, "Dad, can Javi see that his sweater is blue?"

"Yes, but his eyes are different than ours. We have retinas."

"What's that?" Oz asked.

"A retina is located in the back of your eye. It contains light-sensitive cells called cones. We have three cones that help us to see colors like red, blue, and green. Dogs have only two cones, so they see mostly blues and greens."

Oz confirmed, "So Javi can see his sweater is blue?"

Yes, I can.

"Yes, he can."

Sarai was disappointed. "But he can't see my dress is red?"

"Javi doesn't see red the same way we do. Your red dress may look brownish."

"I'll be right back," Sarai said as she danced toward her bedroom.

"Javi also has very little sclera, the white of the eye."

Neha and Oz looked at one another and smiled.

"His eyes don't indicate which direction he's looking at like ours do. We have so many cells in the center of our retina. This allows us to see things right in front of us. Not Javi. He can't clearly see what's right in front of him."

My nose helps.

"One step back allows him to see things very differently."

I take one step back.

Neha and Oz laugh.

"What's so funny?" Sarai said, twirling around the living room in a blue dress.

Roger continued, "Sarai, although your eyes are about the same size as Javi's, they sit in front of your face. Javi's eyes are more sideways on his head."

Sarai had lost interest in the one-way conversation. She said, "Javi, where's the blue balloon?"

That's easy.

I went over and pawed the blue balloon.

POP. I broke the blue balloon.

Am I in trouble?

Sarai laughed. "Where's the green balloon?"

Is this a game?

POP.

"Blue, Javi. Blue," Oz called out.

POP. POP.

Neha sat up on the couch while Roger left the room to answer the ringing doorbell. The balloon game ended, not because I popped them all but because my friends showed up. Misty gave me yummy salmon treats. I loved them almost as much as I loved her. Elvis gave me something very important—his G.I. Joe—the only toy he had from his puppyhood.

Elvis reminded me, "Remember, the invisible superhero cape has special powers. It's always protected me."

"I remember," I reminded Elvis.

"What you don't know is that Ron told me that I'd know when to share it forward. I'd be honored to share it with you, Javi. You're the best friend any dog can ask for."

With humility, I tilted my head forward.

Elvis went through the ridiculous, but necessary charade of taking off the tiny invisible cape, placing it over my head, and tying it beneath my collar. He said, "This is a one-size-fits-all cape."

"Okay," I said with 100 percent belief.

"It never comes off, Javi, not until you feel safe, and you're ready to share it with someone else. Okay?"

"Okay, Elvis. Thank you. This is really special."

Even Ali gave me a birthday present.

Wisdom.

"You can do anything you put your mind to," Ali counseled. "If your mind conceives it, and your heart believes it, you can achieve it." He licked me. "We all have greatness inside of us. Fight through the hard times and reveal your greatness. Don't let anything or anybody distract you."

I knew this included my own negative voice and melon collie.

That night, after everyone left my party, Roger put on his coat and announced, "I'll be in the backyard with Javi."

"And me?" Sarai asked sweetly with her eyes.

"Can I come, too?" Oz begged.

Neha called out, "Put on your hat and gloves."

Outside, Roger, Oz and Sarai looked up at the night sky. I was curious. I looked up, too. The full moon was surrounded by so many bright little lights, too many to count.

Oz asked curiously, "Daddy, do people live up there?"

Roger said, "Are you asking me if people live on the moon?"

"The moon or the stars," replied Oz.

Roger said, "There's no proof of that, but many years ago, when I was about your age, three astronauts—Neil Armstrong, Buzz Aldrin, and Michael Collins—visited the moon. Neil Armstrong was the first man ever to walk on the moon." Roger pointed a tubular thingamajig toward the sky and said, "Here, Oz. Take a look through the lens of this telescope."

Oz put his eye against it and said, "I can't see anything."

Roger laughed. "I'm sorry, my mistake. It's backward, so everything is smaller." He turned the telescope around and put one eye against the end of it. "Now take a look. The faint glow of the moon and the stars will appear much bigger."

"Wow, Daddy. I can see the stars."

"Can I see?" Sarai chimed in.

Roger asked, "Do you see any people?"

"No," Oz said with disappointment. "I don't see any people."

"Let your sister take a look."

I barked.

Sarai looked up at the sky and giggled. "No people or dogs, Javi, just the faint glow of the stars."

A few weeks later, Ali went over the Rainbow Bridge. He was sixteen years old. Elvis joined him the following winter. He was only ten years old. Roger said, "Great Danes live on average for only eight to ten years because they have heart issues."

Elvis's heart was too big.

THE MIDDLE

"You'll never get the dog
that you want.
You'll always get the dog
that you need."

—Cesar Millan

14
Javi

I T'S NOW 2008.

Through the years I've experienced the sun showers of spring, ran through summer's high grass, buried myself in the colorful leaves of fall, and plunged through many winter snowstorms. I recently had two of my bottom teeth removed. My nine-year-old tongue, with its heart-shaped birthmark, now pokes through the empty space. Mama had warned me about this.

I'm learning to accept the things I cannot change.

It's a blustery February morning. My family packs suitcases for their trip and sends me off to stay with Daadee and Daada—Neha's mom and dad. On nice days, they leave me in the backyard because they don't want any more accidents inside their house. On rainy days, I'm allowed to roam only in the room with the window on the ceiling. The window is so high up that all I can see is the sky.

If I stand in the middle of the room and look up at the window, I can see the rain and snow fall, and I can watch the birds and planes fly high in the sky. If I look down, I can recognize every wooden floorboard that creaks in this room. There used to be a rug, but now it's gone because of me. Since we said goodbye to the rug, I've spent most days outside in their backyard. At one time, the backyard had been gloriously fun, but now it seems like a prison.

I dig beneath the white fence and sneak away to get a closer look at two humans walking down the street. The first human smells yummy, like vanilla and cinnamon sugar. She's wrapped in a coat that covers her entire body, including her head. Her hands are tucked deep into pockets like my medicine when it's hidden deep inside peanut butter.

The second human is big and smells like sweat. He wears black pants and a black and white jacket. He waddles like a penguin and struggles to keep up with the lady. She sees me. Her eyes are big dark-chocolate flying saucers. Right below her eyes is her sunny smile.

My entire face smiles back. "Hi lady," I bark. My tail wags as we get closer and closer. I try to emulate her purposeful gait. I love it when she picks me up and holds me against her soft coat.

Penguin calls out, "Don't get too attached, Tali. You know he belongs to somebody."

Lady Tali says to me, "It's okay, precious. Apparently, you've lost your way. Don't worry. We'll find your family."

Kiss. Kiss. Kiss.

Lady Tali holds me tighter and says, "You are so adorable."

Everything I smell has a history. For example, I can smell that her gloves had held the hands of many children, her boots had climbed several mountains, and the scarf around her face not only protected her from the wind and snow but also caught countless tears. These objects know things, and they're here to teach me. All I have to do is smell them.

In her touch, I sense her kindness. I'm 100 percent certain that she can take care of me. She carries me in her arms for many blocks as Penguin waddles close behind. Soon the three of us walk through a door on the side of a house.

"Welcome to my home office, little man." She puts me down and allows me to roam about.

Penguin says, "Bye, Tali. Bye, dog."

Goodbye, Penguin.

I don't smell any other dogs. I do smell a cat, but it's an old smell. Lady Tali puts down a bowl of water and a plate of food.

I love sweet potato.

I eat all of the potato but spit out the green stuff.

Ptooey.

"I'm sorry you don't like spinach. This is all I have. If I had known you were coming, I would have baked a cake." Lady Tali laughs.

Could she really bake a cake? I wonder.

We go outside where a white fence surrounds the yard. In one corner, there's a small body of water—a pond. I'm surprised to see all of the colorful fish, bigger than I am, swimming underneath the partially frozen water. I lick my lips.

Lady Tali says, "That's Nemo, Dory, Marlin, Bubbles, and Gill."

Ugh, knowing their names ruined my sushi fantasy.

After I pee, we go back inside the warm house. First, we play, "Tickle, Tickle." Tali's long fingernails gently touch my skin, and goose bumps form, and travel up and down my paws and then my belly—hysterical! Then we play "Get the Sponge," which I don't get. "Get the Orange," which I can't get because it's too big to fit into my mouth. And finally, we play "Get the Marble," which is fun until it disappears. The best part is when she brushes my hair. I love the way the comb feels on my skin. The finale is me pretending to be a supermodel. Tali takes photos of me until I fall asleep.

The ringing of the doorbell wakes me.

"Tali?" It's a familiar voice.

"Yes. Hi. Please come in."

"Hi. I'm Roger. I guess you can say I'm Javi's father."

Roger!

"Hi, Javi. Were you a good boy?"

Yes, I was. Can I stay?

"I'm sorry for any inconvenience. This isn't the first time Javi escaped from my in-laws' backyard."

Could we not discuss me in front of me?

Tali says, "Javi was a very good boy."

I go to my lady and wag my tail.

Thank you for everything.

Tali half smiles and says, "Bye, Javi. I'm going to miss you."

I can smell things humans can't, like sadness—melon collie. I can tell that Tali's a lady who's hard to reach. I'd bet only the strongest, bravest, and most worthy dog could get to know her. I know I can reach her. I'm a superhero.

Roger says, "Let's go, Javi."

My ears lower as separation anxiety sets in. I sit down by Tali's feet. I stare at her, hugging her with my eyes. "I love you," I bark as I knock on the door to her heart, not too loud because I don't want to frighten her, but not too soft because I want her to hear me.

Roger says, "He's been with Neha and me for nine years, but it appears that he's more attached to you."

"He's not more attached to me," my lady says. "He's just aware that I need him more."

A week passes or maybe it's two. There's no sign of my lady. Another week comes and goes or maybe it's two. I crave the unmistakable sweet smell of vanilla and cinnamon sugar.

"Awoooooooooooooooooooo!"

Another dog howls back. I wonder if he, too, is missing Tali. I can't get her out of my head. I feel an unexplainable connection to her. Perhaps we share an invisible umbilical cord with the universe.

Although my mind wrestles with other images, Tali keeps cropping up every third frame. Her big brown eyes and smile are slipping away. As time erases the details of her face, I become stuck in a web of negativity. I chew Neha's shoes, tear up toilet paper and leave scraps all over the house. I even break into the kitchen garbage bag. I haven't done this in years. I become territorial again. When I'm not demarcating and defending my borders by peeing in the house, I'm contemplating it. And then the day comes when I pee on the new area rug.

I cry out to Mama, "Awoooooooooooooooooooo!"

She answers me. Not out loud, but inside my heart, deep in my soul. She warns me. "Ignore the negative voices and melon collie. Don't open the door."

15
Javi

Neha's cooking *Chana Dal,* which is stewed chickpeas and lentils blended with turmeric, saffron, and other Indian spices. Her neck and shoulder are crooked, hugging the phone. "Hello, is this Tali?"

I listen to every word. My tail races back and forth.

"My name is Neha." She clears her throat nervously. "My husband Roger picked up our dog, Javi, four months ago."

Tali doesn't know why Neha's calling, but I do. These past few months Neha prayed for patience as the chaos erupted around her. Three-year-old Louie's toys clutter every surface, his drawings are pinned to the fridge, and his crayon scribbles decorate the walls. Eleven-year-old Oz is involved in afterschool baseball, and thirteen-year-old Sarai skipped a grade and is now in high school.

There are six baskets of dirty clothes sitting on top of the broken washing machine, and there's a sink full of dirty dishes.

Neha sits at the kitchen table with her cold cup of coffee and her uneaten slice of toast covered with hummus. Her half-opened robe displays her satin nightgown, and her hair is coming undone from her loose ponytail. Sarai's screaming that she has no clean underwear, but Neha can't hear her over the turned-up volume on the TV, and Louie's deafening drumming of metal spoons over pots and pans. I don't help at all. I start to bark.

Neha's voice is loud. "Tali, can you hold on for a minute?" Neha rubs her eyes as the banging gets louder. "LOUIE, STOP IT!"

Louie, wearing his footed pajamas, cries as he runs over to Neha. She picks him up and sits him on her lap. With her free hand, she massages her forehead before she covers her eyes.

I stop barking—mostly because I want to hear the conversation, but I can only hear Neha's part.

"Thank you for holding, Tali."

~~Paws~~. Pause.

Neha says, "Thank you for asking. Right now, my life's like a three-legged stool. I'm struggling for balance."

I watch her move her jaw from side to side.

Neha takes a deep breath and says, "I'm calling because we were wondering if you were in a position to take care of Javi."

Silence.

"Oh yes, he's fine," Neha says without smiling.

I'm now lying down on the wooden floor, under the wooden table surrounded by wooden chairs. There used to be a glorious rug, but they recently sent it away with my scent.

Mama taught me that everything happens for a reason. She said, "Be present in the moment and accept your fate."

Neha's voice cracks. "No, not dog sitting. We were wondering if you wanted him."

More silence.

"Yes, he's fine. I'm just overwhelmed with three kids. The youngest is a handful."

Sarai, Oz , and Louie.

"Yes. That's why we're hoping that you can take Javi."

Pause.

Neha cries and struggles to speak. "Thank you, Tali. Thank you so much. July first is perfect. We'll see you in five days."

One by one, my toys pile up in my crate.

Hey, whaddaya think you're doing with that?

I rescue Allie Gator.

Mine, mine, mine!

A sequence of events soon follows: Roger goes outside with my crate, Neha snivels as she lifts me up, and Sarai and Oz sob. "Goodbye, Javi."

Where're ya going? I wonder. *You're all so emotional.*

Roger returns. "Say goodbye. We have to go."

Goodbye. See you later.

Roger hooks the leash to my collar. Out we go. I pee right away. "Good boy, Javi." He picks me up and kisses my forehead.

I've peed a billion times. Why all this pomp and circumstance now? He puts me into the car.

Hey, what's my bed doing here? I wonder. *My toys? My food?*

Then it hits me. They're not going anywhere—I am. Now I cry.

I'll be a good boy. I won't pee in the house anymore.

"It's okay, Javi. Don't cry. Tali will take good care of you."

Tali?

I stop crying.

Tali!

She meets us outside.

Hiiiiiiiiiiii, my lady.

I follow her up the steps to the front door, not the side door like the first time I went to her house. Inside are more steps.

"Don't be lazy, Javi," Roger says. "Up you go."

I can't believe he calls me lazy in front of my lady. Up I go to look around while Roger puts my toy-filled crate, bag of food, and bed in the spacious living room. I smell the blend of the furniture polish with the fresh air coming in from the open windows. A lavender scent lingers from the freshly vacuumed carpet. The television hanging on the living room wall plays soft music while the near-boiling teapot in the kitchen is getting ready to scream.

I bark, "Where's Allie Gator?"

"Well, I guess that's it," Roger says at the top of the steps.

I bark again, "Where's Allie Gator?"

"You'll be okay, Javi," Roger says.

Humans love to say, "You'll be okay." Or maybe they just need to hear it.

"I WANT ALLIE GATOR!" I bark allowing melon collie to introduce my temper tantrum.

"I'd better go. I'm sure he'll be fine in a few minutes."

I bark again, "I'd be fine right now if I had Allie Gator."

"Thank you, Tali. I don't know what else to say."

"Thank you," my lady says. "Everything will be fine."

Roger goes down the steps and opens the door.

I must have left Allie Gator in the car.

I run down the steps, to the car and paw at the car's back door.

"JAVI!" Roger calls out.

Tali asks, "Did he leave something in the car?"

Roger walks over to the car. "I don't think so."

"Why not double-check?" says my lady from the stoop.

Roger opens the back door. I jump in, grab Allie Gator, jump back down, dash up the front steps and back into the house. I sit at the foot of the steps with Allie Gator in my mouth.

Please, please, please, carry me up the steps.

"So long, Tali. I can see that you have a knack for getting inside Javi's head. You definitely get him, so now you got him."

Tali laughs and says, "Bye, Roger. We'll see you soon."

The car door closes. The engine starts and becomes softer and softer as it travels farther away.

Tali scoops me up and carries me up the six steps.

Yippee!

16
Javi

I DON'T KNOW HOW TO MAINTAIN MY HAPPINESS. I'M AFRAID IF I stay too long, Tali will see my flaws and not want me anymore, like Neha and Roger. Mama warned me that fear and negative thoughts make me vulnerable to melon collie.

Tali's home doesn't have any little humans. It's quiet—very quiet.

We share morning walks and bedtime prayers. She rarely leaves me alone for more than a long nap, but when she does, she leaves the TV on to keep me company. To keep me busy and entertained, Tali hides my favorite treats. To retrieve them, I have to either stand up on my hind legs or squat all the way down to the floor.

I soon realize that my treats aren't the only thing that Tali hides. She hides something else—truth. Tali sometimes smiles when she's sad and cries when she's happy. It's very confusing. I trust one thing and one thing only—human scent. Smells don't lie.

Stress releases certain chemicals in humans called hormones. Increased blood flow brings these hormones to the surface of the skin where their odor is released. I learned this from watching Dr. Oz on TV. I also learned that laughter lowers this stress hormone and makes humans feel much better.

To make Tali laugh, I put my head between her and her book and play Peekaboo with her. Her laughter is like music. She reads out loud. I wonder if this is a human thing.

Are you reading to me? I wonder.

"Dear God, do You love dogs? Is it on purpose that Your names are spelled the same, only in reverse?" Tali smiles at me and says, "God must love dogs."

She shifts her position in the chair and pats her outer thigh. I go to her and recline alongside her leg. "Listen to this, Javi," she says as she continues to read out loud from her book. "'Animals were created ahead of humans to teach them humility. In Genesis, we learn that God told Adam and Eve to give all the animals their Hebrew names. The names they chose were precisely accurate so as to capture the essence of each animal into a name that truly revealed its soul.' Javi, you are so special."

I am?

"'When humans feed their animals before the family, children learn that animals are special.'"

Thank you for always feeding me first even though there are no children here.

Tali continues reading. "'Our love for animals can serve as a guide to help people become more loving for all mankind. In this way, animals can serve as our teachers.'"

I can be a teacher?

"Javi, you're teaching me devotion, loyalty and unconditional love. Are you ready for the finale?"

Finales are usually big. Is this big?

"The Hebrew name for a dog is *kelev,* which is derived from the words *kulo lev* or 'all heart.' Going back to Adam and Eve naming the animals, I think that the Hebrew name for a dog, *kelev,* was perfectly symbolic of a dog's loving soul. Javi, you're all heart."

Can the little heart on my tongue be a miracle?

I'm not sure why Tali shares these deep thoughts with me. Perhaps she's lonely or maybe she believes, like I do, that I'm in training to become a little boy. I'd like to believe that she believes that I truly understand it all.

The next day, I definitely witness a miracle. Tali's cleaning the house: dusting the furniture, mopping the floors, and vacuuming the carpet. Suddenly, I watch her suck up a fly with the big machine. There's no doubt about it. I see it with my own two eyes. I see the big machine eat the fly until it's gone, completely gone!

Tali takes the machine outside and opens its mouth until it spits out the fly, unharmed. With my own eyes, I watch the fly flutter away.

"Who did, who did, who did, who did, who did swallow Jo- Jo-Jonah?"

I used to like the singing, but I didn't believe the story.

"Whale did, whale did, whale did, whale did, whale did swallow Jo- Jo- Jonah."

I've changed. I believe the story. I didn't used to believe in miracles. I do now.

17
Binah

I'LL NEVER KNOW IF JAVI STOPPED WRITING FOR A FEW YEARS OR if I lost some pages, but I now know how Javi met Mommy, who his first family was, and how he changed to believe in miracles.

Me: "Why is it that no matter how many times we tell ourselves that we're going to change, we often give up?"

Cooper: "Who cares?"

Me: "Please don't say that, Cooper. Don't even think that."

Cooper: "Why not?"

Me: "Not caring is the most negative thought we can have. It means that melon collie has been activated. And because we're all connected, what *you* say can affect how *we* feel."

Cooper: "Unless you don't care."

Me: "Daze, do you know how to deal with a difficult dog?"

Daisy: "Is this a joke?"

Me: "No."

Daisy: "I give up anyway."

Me: "You give them more love because acting out is a cry for help. So from now on, Cooper, we'll assume that your secret is that you need more love and attention."

Daisy: "Friends shouldn't keep secrets. I want to share mine because I want help. I'd like to stop peeing inside the house."

Chloe: "That's not really a secret, Daisy."

Daisy gave Chloe a long stare.

Chloe: "Okay, my turn. I'd like to stop biting my tail."

Cooper: "I guess I'd like to stop obsessing over socks. There, I said it."

Me: "I'd like to get rid of my negative voice so that melon collie will stay asleep forever."

Daisy: "That's a hard one, Binah."

Me: "They're all hard, Daze, but we can change. When we succeed in changing our thoughts, then we'll succeed at changing our actions, and we'll grow."

Daisy: "I'll do whatever I need to do, not only to *get* through my challenges, but to *grow* through them."

Cooper: "Me too."

Chloe: "Me three."

Me: "Well said. Count me in, too. Me four."

18
Javi

W E WALK EVERY MORNING AND NIGHT. SOMETIMES WE ALSO walk in the afternoon. Once in a while, Tali takes me on actual smell walks where I inhale many exciting molecules: the grass, the flowers, and even the bugs. It's like human sightseeing. I watch bunnies eat the grass and squirrels jump from branch to branch. I listen to birds chirp, horns honk, and neighborhood kids laugh.

I eat two meals every day, play a little during the day, and snuggle up with Tali at night. Sometimes when Tali reads in bed from a book that she balances on her thighs, I drift off to sleep in the tented space between her bent knees and feet until she snaps the book shut.

I love how Tali calls my name before she speaks to me.

"Javi?"

Yeah?

"Are you ready to go out?"

No.

She slips my head into Blue Sweater before she puts on her own coat. After our walk, she pulls off Blue Sweater, "Say, bye-bye Blue Sweater."

Bye-bye Blue Sweater.

Then comes sleepy time.

"Good night, *mi amore*."

"Good night, my lady."

Kiss. Kiss. Kiss.

"Javi, say hello to Aunt Kim."

Hello, Aunt Kim.

"Hello, Javi." Aunt Kim puts out her hand to pet me but has second thoughts and pulls it away before I get to sniff it.

"Javi, Aunt Kim and I are going to bake *challah* together."

I love the way the house smells when Tali bakes bread. I watch them mix wet ingredients with dry ingredients before turning on the loud machine.

"We've got an hour to let the dough rise," Tali says to me like I'm her assistant, her sous chef.

While Tali and Aunt Kim sit in the dining room talking about adoption, I sit in the kitchen, guarding the *challah*. With my very own eyes, I watch it double in size. After the timer goes off, Tali punches the *challah* with her fist, and the whole thing collapses.

I'm horrified.

Aunt Kim says, "Life is filled with obstacles that sometimes throw a punch and knock us down."

"I appreciate the analogy, Aunt Kim, but I've been waiting so long. The paperwork was completed two years ago. The agency social worker finalized her home study report, and this is the third time I was matched with a baby and it fell through."

Baby? Did you say, baby?

Tali whispers, "Do you think it's because I'm single?"

Aunt Kim shakes her head and says, "No."

Tali says, "I know. Bread is punched down only so it can rise even higher."

Sounds deep.

Aunt Kim hugs Tali, "That's a lesson for all of us. You'll see. You'll get your match. It will be a match beyond your wildest dreams."

After Aunt Kim leaves carrying a bag of bread that smells yummy, Tali tells me the secret ingredient for all things to rise.

Love.

19
Javi

T ALI IS AN EARLY RISER. SHE GETS UP WHEN IT'S STILL DARK and either goes downstairs to her office to work or into the gym to push metal plates up and down with her arms and legs. I, on the other hand, wake up when the natural light comes through the blinds. That's when I get up and head over to the top of the steps. It amazes me how she knows I'm there even though I don't bark. I swear I don't make a peep. She just knows.

She'll call out from downstairs, "Are you up, my precious little man?"

It's equally rewarding if I wait in bed until Tali tiptoes into the bedroom. I keep my eyes closed pretending to be asleep, even though I know that she knows I sleep with my eyes open. Yeah, I know, creepy, but true. I hold back my giggles until she reaches my side of the bed, tickles my tummy, and sings, "Uppy, uppy, little puppy." So, you see, either way it's a win-win for me. And if Tali were writing this entry, she'd insist that it's a win-win for her.

We usually take our morning walk by eight, but this morning, Tali didn't wake me up until nine. After our morning ritual of "Tickle, Tickle," Tali scoops me up out of bed and scoots me over to my water bowl in the kitchen. She puts ice cubes in it because Roger told her that I loved ice-cold water. It's true, I do.

Despite the uninterrupted sunshine, it's a cool morning. My nose adjusts to the crisp fresh air that quickly fills my lungs. Every few steps of our walk, I turn all the way around and look back to make sure that Tali's still behind me. After walking our mile and stopping at all my usual pit stops, we're nearly home.

Suddenly Tali tenses up, drops my poopy bag, and screams, "NOOOOOO!"

Several things happen at the speed of light. I feel a strong tug on my neck as I hear my collar rip off. I catch a glimpse of my name tag flying through the air. I'm airborne, but soon enough I hit the ground. All the while I never take my eyes off Tali, who never takes her eyes off the big, mean dog who attacked us.

I'll call him TIM (Terrorist in Motion).

I see Tali's eyes bug out, and that alone scares me. There's no way I'm interested in seeing whatever she's looking at. Her mouth is wide open, frozen in time, as she runs toward me. I'm paralyzed.

I'm telling you, from the moment I see Tali's eyes bugging out, I can't move. Finally, Tali dives on top of me, but lands on me like a roll of soft paper towels.

"STOP!" yells a deep voice.

Not only do I hear Tali's heart hammering, but I feel it. I also smell her stress hormones. My teeth are clenched, my chest is tight and my body quivers. With his built-up ego and his broken-down spirit, TIM bites me. I feel the fresh wound sting as it seeps into my flesh. Although I don't actually see it, I'm guessing the owner grabs TIM. When Tali moves off of me, I immediately jump up and run like the wind.

Tali yells, "JAVI, STOP!"

Somewhere down the block, I stop running. Tali catches up to me, kneels down, and gently touches me all over. "Are you okay?" She lifts me up, "Oh, thank God you're not bleeding."

I'm not bleeding? I heard my skin break, and I feel my white blood cells coming together to fight infection and build a scab.

With her heart beating like a metronome on steroids, Tali carries me back to that place.

Whaddaya crazy, lady?

The man says, "Are you okay? Your leg is bleeding."

Tali's bleeding?

I thought TIM bit *me.*

"I'll be fine, but I'm taking my little guy to the vet."

"Whatever it costs, I'll pay for it. I'm very sorry."

Tali picks up my broken collar and leash and carries me home. After she takes off her broken pants and washes her boo-boo, we go to Dr. Noah. He confirms that there's nothing wrong with me. From there, we go to a store that allows dogs to shop with their humans. As we walk toward the store's entrance, the door whooshes open by itself. Her fascinating scent blows into my face.

"Misty!" I bark with excitement. What a sight for sore eyes.

"Hi, Javi. Do you like my new haircut?"

"You look beautiful, Misty." My bark is loud because I'm still excited to see her.

"What are you doing here?"

Now, I whisper. "Uh, I just rescued Tali from this, um, gigantic monster, and she's, uh, here to get me a prize."

"You're like a superhero, Javi."

I feel proud for about five seconds. Then the shame settles in. I keep the small talk going so Misty can't hear Tali tell her dad what really happened. After I kiss Misty goodbye, Tali walks me down the yummy aisle. In a blue basket that she carries in her crooked arm, she puts not one, not two, but *three* bags of treats. From another aisle, she adds a squeaky toy, an adjustable leash, and a red collar, which looks brownish to me. She picks out a heart-shaped name tag and a charm that says, "Little Angel."

"Javi Stark. How does that sound?"

I love it.

Together, we go to the engraving machine and wait.

"It's official. Javi Stark." Tali says as she attaches my new name tag to my new collar and fastens it around my old neck.

I'm happy to be Javi Stark. I love that moment, and I play it over and over again in my head. What I don't love is what happens when we get home.

I consider myself a curious dog on a never-ending journey of discovery. I'm usually okay if I don't know what's around the corner. We go for another one of our usual walks. As we round the corner, I freeze. I know exactly where we are. I've been here before, and I'm not a fan. I smell Tali's apprehension like it's burned meat, which I would still eat, and growl at TIM's house. I smell my own anger rising like the yeast cells thriving on cinnamon sugar, releasing carbon dioxide and alcohol and causing the sweet bread to rise.

I learned this from watching the cooking channel.

As Tali knocks on the door, the rumbling growl and the threatening snarl emerge from my mouth. I'm aware that my negative voice and melon collie are knocking. Mama had warned me about them. I choose to ignore them. Instead, I inhale courage and exhale fear. The man opens the door, gives Tali money and a squeaky toy, apologizes again and shuts the door. That's it. We head back home.

Later that night, before bed, Tali whispers, "I'm sorry for the trauma we experienced today."

Me too.

Tali whispers again, "I love you, *mi amore*. Sweet dreams."

Tali needs me, but I also need her. For the entire night, I keep one eye on my restless Tali and one eye out the window. I stare at the awesome sky with its full moon and shining stars.

Soon I whisper, "Tali, are you sleeping?"

No answer except for an occasional soft snore.

Despite feeling exhausted, I fight my body's need for sleep. I allow my negative thoughts to flood my brain and activate melon collie. Both my head and belly ache as I listen to my negative voice come alive.

"Javi, you're not a superhero like Misty said. You should feel ashamed of yourself. You should've protected Tali. That's what real superheroes do."

Outside, the lightning flashes, and the thunder roars. As flashbacks of TIM attacks my mind, I jump on top of Tali but not nearly as gently as she landed on me earlier that day.

Tali covers me with her "champion" T-shirt and sings to me until I finally fall asleep.

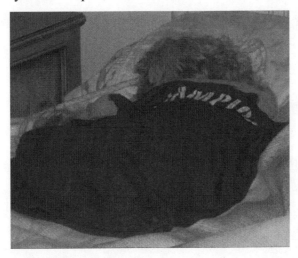

20
Javi

SOON AFTER TALI GOT HER BOO-BOO, I GET ONE OF MY OWN. WE are back at the doctor's office. This time I notice things that I hadn't noticed the first time we were here. Against the wall is a glass cage filled with water where colorful fish, much smaller than the ones in Tali's pond, swim. Hanging from every wall, behind pieces of glass, are pictures of cats, dogs, and birds frozen in time. At the far end of the room is a cage with a talking bird inside.

Yup, you heard me, a talking bird.

"Where's it hurt?" chirps the bird. "Kiss the boo-boo."

Fascinating.

"Hello. What's wrong? Where's it hurt? Kiss the boo-boo."

Is he a miracle?

"Hello. What's wrong? Where's it hurt? Kiss the boo-boo."

Is he broken?

I tap my tail on the floor several times. Blood races to my cheeks. I suck my teeth and sigh.

"Javi Stark," the lady dressed all in white calls out.

"Javi Stark," the bird calls out. "Javi Stark."

I follow Tali and the lady into a room where I'm happy to recognize Dr. Noah in his white coat.

He's soft-spoken. "Hi, Javi. How are you today?" Dr. Noah says as he puts me down on a cool metal table.

I sniff around and smell other dogs.

With gentle hands he touches my body, mostly my boy parts and says, "It's best to be neutered around six months." Although he uses big words like "enlarged prostate" and "consequences," it's Tali's scent that scares me. Her stress hormones are active again.

Dr. Noah and Tali set a date.

Is it for lunch?

No. It's not.

After my surgery, Dr. Noah sends me home with a toy so big Tali can't carry it, so I have to wear it around my head.

Although I never figure out exactly how to play with it, I think it's like human bumper cars because I keep banging into things, and I bounce back unharmed. Tali plays with it too. Each time she speaks to me, her words echo into my ears.

"I love you, Javi . . . Javi . . . Javi."

Tali brushes my hair, gives me treats, sings to me, gives me treats, massages my body, and give me treats. Soon enough, I'm back to normal.

In our yard, I play with a rotting squirrel corpse. Dogs love this smell. Humans? Not so much. Within seconds, Tali hoists me to her waist and carries me under one arm, sideways, my head drooping downward. Everything is now at a lopsided, dizzying angle. She rushes me up the steps and into the tub. Warm water whooshes past my ears. The clear water that first touches my body collides with the dark grime on my body and races down the drain. The foul-smelling soap that Tali uses lingers in my fur long after being rinsed off. I'm ashamed of myself. At nine-and-a-half years old, I still have the self-control of a puppy. After my bath, Tali wraps me up tightly in a towel, like I'm a present. She holds me in her lap and sings to me. Not a terrible punishment.

After she puts me down on the floor, I shake myself from head to tail. Water pellets ricochet off the glass shower door onto the floor. Still wet, I race down the carpeted hallway, up onto the couch, off the couch, up the carpeted hallway, up onto the bed, off the bed and back down the carpeted hallway. I franticly rub my back, my shoulders, and my face against the carpet. I leave the butt cheeks for the grand finale.

At night as we sleep, Tali's fingers rest on my paw or maybe it's my paw that rests on her fingers.

21
Javi

AFTER BREAKFAST, ENTICING ODORS SWIRL OUT WITH TALI'S words, "You are a very special soul, Javi. I know you can do this." She pushes the buttons on the phone and waits. "Hi. I'm interested in the dog certification program."

Pause.

"Yes, I can hold." Tali looks at me at asks, "Do you want a job?"

I do if I can taste-test cookies.

I had watched dogs on TV sit and eat. I know I could do that.

Pick me, pick me.

"His name is Javi Stark."

I love to hear her say my name.

"Yes." She looks at me and smiles. "He's a very good boy."

Thanks, Tali.

"He's nine." Tali looks away as she underestimates my age by half a year. I can tell that her smile disappears. "He's a very young nine-year-old." Her smile is back.

Good thinking, Tali.

"Okay. I'll fill out the paperwork online, get his license, confirm his vaccines, and take his photo. Thank you."

"Javi, you're applying to be a pet therapist. Try to smile, *mi amore.* Nobody will hire an angry little man."

Kiss. Kiss. Kiss.

"You know what, Javi? We'll get you a haircut tomorrow and then we'll take your photo."

Great idea.

"Besides, it's time for you get your glands squeezed."

You're crazy if you think that's gonna get me to smile.

RULE: Even if your butt itches, do not drag it across the carpet in front of the big humans. They'll likely take you to some freak groomer who'll squeeze the beejeebies out of your tushy. It's definitely okay to tushy walk in front of the little humans. They'll laugh, and if you're lucky, they'll even give you a treat.

After my haircut, I take my official pet therapist photo.

"Javi, you look so handsome," Tali says with a smile as big as the day we first met.

I don't mind the polka-dot bandana, but I'm not thrilled to see my bottom teeth missing.

Tali puts the papers, photo, and something she refers to as a check, which looks nothing like a ✓, into an envelope and licks it with a scrunched-up face.

Can I lick it?

She puts the envelope into her bag and then zips it up.

I guess not.

Tali talks into the phone. "I mailed Javi's papers six weeks ago."

Pause.

"Javi Stark."

I love sharing the same last name with Tali.

"Yes. Thank you."

Longer pause.

"I'm on hold, Javi."

Thanks for telling me.

"Yes, I'm still here."

Very short pause.

"He's nine. Can you please move him up the list?"

Another short pause.

"Yes, I can hold." Tali winks at me. "I'm on hold."

If you're on hold, then I'm on hold.

"Tomorrow, Saturday?" Tali gives me the thumbs-up sign.

I love the thumbs-up sign. I wish I had thumbs.

"Yes, we'll be there." Tali's excited. "Thank you."

I sit up with my ears perked and my tail wagging.

Tali puts down the phone. "Well, *mi amore*, they're testing in our neighborhood tomorrow."

Testing? Tomorrow? What does this mean? Am I being tested? Is there a book to read? I like reading.

Tomorrow turns into today. Tali parks the car in this big empty field. We walk in the pouring rain up a hill to a tent where six humans and two dogs sit. A lady asks Tali questions: "How old is Javi? May I see his paperwork? Did he ever bite anyone?"

Tali responds, "Nine, of course, and never."

Soon after that my test begins.

On command, I have to sit, stay, and walk past two dogs without barking. I then have to walk past six humans without getting excited and stay calm despite loud music playing, dogs growling, and humans screaming. I'm then told to walk past food and leave it, stay calm while being forcefully petted and sit still on a man's lap while he sits in a wheelchair. It's all pretty easy until the lady tells Tali to walk away.

You can do it, Tali.

"Stay, Javi," Tali says.

I stay.

I'm cool.

Tali slowly walks away, turns around and says, "Stay, Javi."

I hear you, Tali. You're doing great. Come right back.

She walks farther away, turns around once more and says with love in her eyes, "Stay, *mi amore*," and then she disappears.

Is this a game? You're coming back, right? Oh jeez, we should've practiced this one at home. This part of the test seems like FOREVER.

The lady says, "Okay, it's been five minutes. C'mon out."

FIVE MINUTES? Tali! Tali! Tali!

Tali says, "Stay, Javi. Good boy!" I stay until Tali says, "Come."

Oh my gawd. This last part was so hard.

We wait and wait and wait. The uncertainty of my future is killing me. And then . . .

"Congratulations. Javi has a gentle temperament. He's very sweet, outgoing, and doesn't get too excited."

Does this mean that I passed?

Tali hugs me and says, "Javi, you passed."

I can smell Tali's happy hormones.

Yay!

The same lady says, "You'll receive Javi's working papers, therapy dog tag, and bandana in the mail. He can begin working in whichever participating organizations you choose."

Back at the car, Tali hugs and kisses me even though I'm soaking wet from the rain and covered in mud.

Tali's voice cracks. "You are so special, Javi. I'm so proud of you. Now, you get to help people. Some will need to pet you, others will need to just see you, and still others will only need to feel your energy."

22
Javi

TALI SOFTENS MY STIFF "THERAPY DOG" BANDANA JUST IN TIME for my first job at the nursing home. Like any health professional, I've changed the names of my patients to respect their privacy.

Mary's a tiny, maybe four-feet-tall, sixty-year-old woman who sits in a wheelchair. She has webbed hands. Her nail-less fingers are all attached. She can't see, speak, hear, or smell, but she does have her sense of touch and is happy to pet me. Tali's smile confirms that I'm doing a good job. Mary smiles for many visits, until one day she's no longer at the nursing home. A nurse tells us that Mary passed away. I know this means that she went over the Rainbow Bridge.

A week later, I meet Jerry. He's been at the nursing home for five years and never played with other humans. I don't know his age, but like Mary, he sits in a wheelchair. He can see and hear, but he can't make words, only sounds. One day, he gestures with his hands for me to come closer.

"Do you want to pet Javi?" Tali asks Jerry.

He nods, reaches out his arms, and waves his hands.

"Javi, Jerry wants to pet you. This is wonderful. Maybe, after he pets you, you can gently kiss his hand?"

I can do that.

Jerry pets me and quickly moves his hand away. He pets me a second time. His hand is mechanical, like a robot. He rubs my head with his flat palm, and then again, he quickly moves his hand away. He pets me a third time and keeps his hand on my forehead. I wait for the right moment. I lick my lips. He moves his hand slightly, and I kiss his wrist just as he pulls it away. He laughs. Everybody laughs. I don't need to look at Tali to know that I did a great job.

Jerry says, "Ja-veee." Although he only says it once, everyone agrees that it's amazing to hear his voice. I visit with Jerry for several weeks before he, too, goes over the Rainbow Bridge. I bet he couldn't wait to tell Mary what a good boy I am.

Marty is an angry man who can't control his temper because something happened to his brain. Tali kept us away from him for a long time because she didn't want us to get hit by his flailing arms or flying spit.

One day, Marty calls out, "Dog."

Guardedly, Tali walks us over to him. Three workers stand nearby as Tali brings me closer to him. Marty raises his hand as if to pet me, but instead he slams his hand down onto my head.

Ouch.

I'm able to blink away the stars, but nothing, not even Tali's love, helps my headache. We never go anywhere near his room or the nursing home again.

I'm excited to start my new job working with little humans at the foster home.

23
Javi

SHE HIDES BEHIND LOTS OF MAKEUP, A COLORFUL WIG, AND A big red nose. She has so many layers on, I can't smell her.

I'm upset and bark, "What did you do with my lady?"

And then I hear her sweet voice. "Hi, *mi amore*."

"Tali? Is that you?"

She removes the nose.

"Tali! Tali! Tali!"

Kiss. Kiss. Kiss.

Only Tali knows that I'll be wearing a similar outfit, minus the wig and big red nose, for my next job.

Inside the office building, clicking heels get louder as the smell of coconut gets stronger.

"You must be Tali," says the coconut-smelling lady in heels.

"Yes, and this is Javi."

"I'm Lee Victors, the adoption agency supervisor." She bends down to rub my head gently. "Hi Javi. You look adorable. Thank you for working with us."

Lee Victors, you smell delicious.

Tali says, "Javi's happy to help. He grew up with three kids."

I miss Sarai, Oz, and Louie.

We walk over to the big shiny gray doors. Seconds after Lee pushes a button, the doors open. What a chilling experience. It's like we walked into a whale's mouth, were swallowed up, and moved inside its belly.

Who did, who did, who did, who did, who did swallow Jo- Jo-Jonah?

And like Jonah, when the ride is over, the mouth opens, and the whale spits us out unharmed. I see everything has changed: the people, the walls, and even the carpet. We follow Lee down a hall, through a door, and then through another door. We stop in front of a room. The door is open. From inside, I hear a calm voice.

"It's okay, Missy."

"I want my mommy," cries, I'm assuming, Missy.

Lee pokes her head inside the door and says, "The advocates are here."

Advocate is a big word.

Tali whispers to me. "You're the advocate, Javi. Your job is to love this little girl."

Got it.

"Missy, look who's here," says Calm Voice.

Missy turns around. "Doggy!" She's very excited.

I love this job.

Lee says, "Would you like to say hi to Javi?"

"Hello, doggy clown," Missy whispers.

Missy's smaller than Louie. Her little hand touches my head, under my cockamamie hat with a pom-pom.

"Sit." Missy points to the floor.

I sit.

Tali winks at me. "Good boy, Javi."

I blink both eyes twice because I don't know how to wink.

"Down. Down." Missy claps her hands.

I lay down. I even roll over, causing Missy to laugh. I roll over again. Her laugh becomes a loud shriek. We play until it's time for Missy to go.

Goodbye, Missy.

One week later, instead of the clown suit, I wear my official "Therapy Dog" bandana and go back to the same building. Although I hear the same clicking heels on the wooden floor, smell the same coconut lotion, and experience the same chilling whale ride, I don't go back to the same room. Nor do I see Missy. Instead, I meet a little boy named Steven. He has dark skin, dark hair, and dark eyes. He's wearing denim overalls.

Where's Missy?

I didn't know that when I said goodbye to Missy that I wouldn't see her again.

Steven says, "Down!"

After I stand up in order to sit down, Lee gives Steven a cookie. I lower my belly to the ground and roll over. Although Steven laughs, I don't get a cookie. When it's time for me to go, I don't say goodbye to Steven because I want to see him again.

Another week passes. It's a different day, a different room and a different child.

What's going on here?

Tali senses my uneasiness. "Javi, don't be sad. These children are here only for a short time. That's a good thing. When they leave, it's because they found a family. Missy and Steven are now with people who love them and will take care of them. We want that for all of these children. Okay?"

Okay.

At the end of the day, my newest friend, Ben, gets two cookies. Two treats for Ben and none for me. That's how life is sometimes. Some dogs are good dogs and get no treats at all. But, I do discover my dual mission: to help humans (big and small) smile and to show that dogs can be part of a loving friendship. We all do better when we're paired with a caring advocate. One dog can't help everyone, but every dog can help someone.

After saying goodbye to many children, Lee gives me a present—a doggy pillow. The picture on the pillow reminds me of my baby sister, Princess Leia. I love this pillow. I'd choose it over 100 cookies.

Tali keeps the pillow on our bed, and I sleep on it every night

24
Javi

TALI HOLDS ONTO THE STEERING WHEEL IN THE FRONT SEAT, and I hold down my blanket in the back seat. Allie Gator sleeps nearby. Tali rolls down my window so I can breathe in the fresh air. I stand up and stick my head outside, my nose forging ahead. The wind blows infinite scent molecules directly into my face. Suddenly, the car hits a bump in the road, and I'm tossed from the light of day into the dark of night.

"Javi?" Tali pulls the car over to the side of the road.

I'm here.

"Are you okay?

I poke my head up. My muffled reply from the floor of the back seat is, "I'll be okay." Everyone likes the way that sounds, even a dog. "Where's Allie Gator?" I bark.

"Alligator didn't move. She's still sleeping."

I love how she understands me.

I jump back up onto the seat while Tali drives to the store where dogs shop with their humans. She picks up my favorite treats and a very short leash.

Back at the car, while I reunite with Allie Gator, Tali wraps the short leash around me and says, "From now on you'll wear a seatbelt just like I do." She closes my door, walks around the front of the car, opens her door, slides into her seat, and turns around to face me. With her phone held high she says, "Look away and act as if you don't know that I'm about to take your picture."

How's this?

"Perfect," Tali says. "Now, let's go visit my family."

Tali wakes me from my nap. "We're here, Javi."

Outside, a lantern-shaped porch light above the door glows brighter as we get closer. I'm mesmerized by this brilliant, magnificent light. I'm unable to break eye contact until I smell something. Can it be the hanging basket overflowing with marigolds? No. That's not it. Can it be the dandelions blooming in the terra-cotta pots? I learned this big word from watching Martha Stewart on TV. Ah, here it is. I smell a dog on one of the flowerpots.

"Don't get any ideas, Javi." Tali says as she pushes a button on the house. The door opens and the smell of yummy food floats outside. I lick at the invisible air hoping to taste what I smell.

Unlike dogs who say hello the normal way, Tali's brother, Joseph, and his wife, Rachel, greet us with waving hands, hugs, and kisses. Four little humans come running over, chanting my name as if I'm a celebrity. It takes me a few seconds to understand their names because they're all talking at once. They're my little cousins.

Erika has long blonde hair, but more importantly, she smells like French fries. Seth, the only boy, smells like hamburgers. Both Dana, who wears her brown curly hair in a braid, and Melanie, the smallest of the litter, who has jet-black curls that twirl around her face, wear the scent of a dog.

Where's the dog?

I sniff, sniff, sniff, sniff each of their paws for treats but find nothing. All four little humans follow me into the kitchen where I smell cooked meat. Hera's helping Andrew, Tali's other brother build a sandwich.

Like Joseph, who has salt-and-peppered hair, Andrew is big. Despite his extra weight, he looks strong, and despite his full head of gray hair with several white hairs lodging into the sides of his temples, he looks young. He bites into his sandwich just after he makes this trumpet-sounding noise with his lips and just before the vein on his neck protrudes. That's when I spot her.

"Hi. I'm Coco. I'm a Cavalier King Charles spaniel."

"Hi, Coco. I'm Javi. I'm a shih tzu."

"I'm six years old," says Coco.

"I'm ten."

"WHOA." Coco's eyes widen. "I weigh twenty pounds. My doctor told my family that I should weigh sixteen pounds. I feel bad when my friends call me fat."

"You're not fat, Coco. You're shapely."

"I have to lose weight. I can't reach the places where I itch, and I'm always out of breath," Coco says trying to catch her breath.

"My mom, Tali, teaches humans to eat healthy. She tells them to eat until they're no longer hungry rather than eat until they're full."

"That's funny, Javi. My dad, Andrew, believes we should eat and never stop because we never know when our next meal will be."

"Coco, you're hysterical. But seriously, exercise is also important. Tali walks me twice a day."

Coco flops onto the floor. "Seriously, Andrew says exercise is for losers. Although my ancestors were athletic and gifted at fetching balls, I don't fetch much of anything. I admit it. I'm lazy, and I love my treats."

"I love treats too," I say.

"Do you want to learn how to get lots of treats?"

"Sure." I'm excited.

"It's simple," Coco says. "Hang out with the little humans."

Dana's first to offer food. "Do you want to taste cottage cheese, Javi?"

It doesn't smell like anything, and it looks like a white turd.

The smallest human, Melanie, says, "It's good, Javi."

I wrinkle my nose, roll it around on my tongue, and spit it out. *I say, nay nay.*

I don't like bananas, peas, or corn either, but I absolutely love the chili dog that Seth gives me.

"Do you want to taste pizza?" Erika puts down a small piece.

I chew and chew and chew. Too much work. Remember, I'm missing a few teeth. I spit it out and give it to Coco. In return, Coco shares her food, water, and even her bed. We get along great.

On the drive home, that chili dog barks out of my butt. I'm not sure who's more disturbed by the unexpected noises, Tali or me.

The following week we take a long drive to visit Tali's parents. The car reeks of the new vanilla air freshener hanging from the rearview mirror. My eyes are closed the entire trip except for when Tali stops the car to let me out to pee. Next thing I know, Tali whispers, "Javi, we're here."

"Where's the dog?" Gramma calls out from the porch.

The dog. I hate that.

I want to say, "I have feelings. Please use my name, Javi. I don't call you 'the human,' 'Tali's mom,' or, as I discover, 'the lady with no treats.'" Instead I bark, "Here I am."

The door opens. A powerful collection of smells float over me.

Gramma says, "Hi, Javi. You're very handsome."

I sniff her hand.

She pats my head. "Hello, pussycat."

No treats combined with being called pussycat. This is not good.

I hope to have better luck with Grampaw. He sits on a chair that has tennis balls on its feet. I wait.

"'Nice to meet you, Javi," says Grampaw.

"Can I have a treat?" I bark.

"Come." Grampaw calls me over. "Good girl." He says rubbing my ears.

Tali laughs. "Dad, Javi is a boy."

Cat, dog, girl, boy. Where's the food?

Gramma calls out, "Who's hungry?"

I am! I am!

Gramma takes a tray of meat out of the oven, puts it on the countertop and leaves the kitchen. I, being the responsible one, stand guard. Whaddaya think happens next? Do you think I:

(a) jump up on the countertop and devour the meat?

(b) jump up on the countertop and knock over the tray, causing the meat to land on the floor?

(c) sit there like an idiot until Gramma comes in and gives me one single cockamamie piece?

The answer is (c).

I wait for more. I look at Gramma, who looks at Tali, and then at Grampaw, who looks at me, and then finally at Tali, who looks back and forth between them. Tali plays a game with Grampaw. She wraps a little blanket around his arm and squeezes the attached black ball which inflates the little blanket.

Interesting. Maybe I can play next?

Tali rattles off some numbers.

Gramma claps. "I told you to stay away from the salt."

This is a stupid game.

Tali puts the toy away. I can't reach it, and I never get to play.

Grown-ups should really learn to share.

Gramma calls out, "Javi, time to eat lunch."

My ears flip back while my tongue, with its heart-shaped birthmark, smacks my lips over and over again like a boxing match. Gramma puts down a small plate of meat, rice, and carrots. It's really good. I eat it in six seconds. I want more. I sit patiently under the table right near Grampaw. I'm on patrol for falling food. I pray for an avalanche.

"Sorry, Javi," Grampaw says. "This is people food."

When I'm a boy, I'll share my food with everyone, even the dog.

I listen to them talk over the sound of their forks and knives hitting their plates.

"Grampaw?"

I'm patient.

"Grampaw?"

Very patient.

"GRAMPAW!"

"Javi, shush." Tali gently scolds me.

I listen to Grampaw eat his food. When I lick his leg his hand appears with scraps of meat. I eat it right from his hand.

Thanks, Grampaw.

After lunch, Grampaw takes us all out for a ride on Silver Boat. While I gaze up at the cloudless sky, the humans put on bulky vests.

Tali secures me onto her lap, and as Silver Boat starts to move, she says, "Look at the water, Javi. Feel the waves."

WEEEEEEEE!

Tali sings, "Row, row, row your boat, gently down the stream. Merrily, merrily, merrily, merrily, life is but a dream."

After the sun goes down, there are a lot of goodbye hugs and kisses. Tali buckles me into the front seat of the car and backs out of the driveway. Affection pours off her hand and onto my fur.

I sleep all the way home.

25
Javi

THANK GOODNESS FOR MORNING RITUALS.

After Tali attaches my leash, we leave from the side door and take the fastest route across the driveway to the sidewalk, where I squat and watch the flood of urine flow past my hind paws and disappear into the cracks of the sidewalk. I always hold some urine in reserve for marking the bushes and hydrants, and I aim high because it's easier for the odor in the urine to be read by others.

I forever sniff new scents by inhaling and exhaling. Sniffing my neighbors' pee is like reading a human text message or the community's bulletin board. HEAR YE! HEAR YE!

I know the writers, their moods and their stories. Old messages are flagged as outdated, but the good ones, like a Pulitzer Prize winning novel, still get read. Poop also holds identifying odors. A chemical from the pea-sized anal gland drops on top of the poop when a dog's afraid. On a windy day, a dog might scratch his message into the ground to ensure the wind doesn't blow it away or the message can travel by airmail across town on the fallen leaves. Finally, like a human who's just joined a dating site, our markings increase when a new dog's in town. These neighborhood dogs have questions. I hope my answers are enough. Here's the best of the best from my recollection.

I got pee mail.

Q: Sometimes when there's not enough food, I eat the cat's food. Is this okay?

A: Eat only your food when it's given to you. Never sneak anyone else's food before they get to it or especially after they throw it up.

Q: My family just adopted a puppy. I was told to be nice. I'm sixteen years old. Why do I have to be nice?

A: It's nice to be nice. And while you're at it, be kind. Be generous. Be of service. The simple message is one of love.

Q: Have you ever tasted bunny poop?

A: Yes, back in the day, but I stopped eating fast food when I moved in with Tali. Nothing compares to her homemade food.

Q: What's the secret to happiness?

A: If you want to be happy for a minute, eat a cookie. If you want to be happy for an hour, get a squeaky toy. If you want to be happy for a month, have your belly rubbed. If you want to be happy forever, always share your love with a human.

Q: I want puppies more than anything. Where are they?

A: More important than getting what we want is getting what we need. This prepares us for long-term happiness. If you're not getting what you want right now, maybe it's because you aren't ready for it. Work hard and don't give up on your dream.

Q: Don Juan is a poopy head. Watch out, girls, he'll be all lovey-dovey with you one day and then ignore you the next.

A: Speaking badly about another may seem harmless in the moment, but what we give, we get in return. Negative thoughts create negative energy. Be careful.

Q: Do you act the same way when humans are watching you or are you a totally different dog when you're alone?

A: I've learned that when my alone behavior is very different from my social behavior, I feel less connected and less fulfilled. I now act as if my human is always watching me.

Q: Where is God?

A: Like the electricity in our home, He's everywhere. You just need to plug in.

Q: When we go over the Rainbow Bridge, do we reunite with our humans or our mamas?

A: The unknown is not understandable, but I choose to believe that we reunite with both.

Q: Do you ever get bored?

A: I'm never bored, not even when my human leaves me alone. I take in the sights: the mailman, a bunny's hippety-hop, cars, and humans. And, let's not forget, there's a lot to be discovered by a sniffing nose and roving tongue.

I bet that when I'm a human boy, I won't be bored either, but if I am, I definitely won't twiddle my thumbs. Perhaps I'll sit in the kitchen until someone, like Tali, takes cookies out of the oven. Or, if I have a brother, I'll pace madly up and down the carpeted hallway in my socks, gathering just enough static electricity to shock him with a touch of my ~~paw~~ finger.

26
Javi

ONE DAY I'M FINE AND THE NEXT DAY, NOT SO MUCH.

I rest my chin on Tali's thigh as she pretends to sleep. Soon enough, I jump off the bed and run out past the bedroom door. At lightning speed, I zigzag up and down the carpeted hallway, and I bark like it's the Fourth of July. Tali races downstairs ahead of me. Like last night and the night before that, she opens the back door just in time. After a few draining moments of throwing up, my nausea fades.

I'm sorry, Tali.

"I'm sorry, *mi amore*." She picks me up, wipes my face with a damp towel, and carries me back to bed. I sleep until daylight peeks through the blinds and then scoot over onto Tali's pillow and rest my furry head against her furry head.

She kisses me. "Are you feeling better, li'l man?"

I feel scared.

My negative voice has activated melon collie, who's now stealing my joy.

Sometimes, when my mind is quiet, I connect with Mama. She'll stand on a wooden bridge or sleep on a metal bridge. One time, she even sat on a colorful bridge made out of Sarai's plastic building blocks. Mama tells me to pay attention. She says, "The lessons are in front of you. Look for the rainbow." The visits happen so fast, I don't have time to ask any questions.

I wake up, sit up, and then flatten my body back down against the cozy bed sheet, trying to get comfortable. Neither Tali nor I can sleep. I follow her into the kitchen. She opens the fridge and pulls out the butter and eggs. She then opens the cabinet and takes out the flour, sugar, vanilla, cinnamon, and chocolate chips. She softens the butter in the microwave, adds the sugar, eggs, and vanilla, then stirs in the dry ingredients and puts many trays of rounded balls of dough into the hot oven. I've watched her do this so many times, I could be her sous chef.

After the house smells like a delicious cookie factory, Tali takes a deep breath, crouches down to my level, holds out her sticky finger, and says, "Dr. Noah said this medicine will help you. I want to believe him."

I willingly lick her finger clean, knowing all too well that the medicinal odor will return to me like a boomerang.

"Good boy, Javi. You are such a good boy."

The digital clock says 4:30 a.m. My bladder wakes me, and I wake Tali. Without complaint, she puts her coat on over her pajamas and slips into her furry boots before quickly shoveling the ankle-high snow that had fallen overnight. She does this so that I, the precious eleven-year-old shih tzu, can pee outside in the cold rather than inside where it's nice and warm.

From behind the sliding glass door, I watch Tali get into a rhythm. Knees bent, lower shovel, push shovel, lift shovel, throw snow, and repeat. In a matter of minutes, she's covered with snowflakes. Then it's my turn. Tali slips me into Blue Sweater and I trample on and quickly color the snow with my pee. Within seconds I, too, am covered with snow and can't walk because the snow quickly hardens under my paws.

"Javi, you look like a snow-covered Ewok." Tali laughs and carries me inside. She defrosts me in the bathroom under the hand dryer mounted on the wall. Yup, you heard me, she has a hand dryer in her house. I feel her love as I dangle from her arms, the snow melting off my body into a puddle on the floor.

Back in bed, I quickly drift off to sleep, but not before Tali whispers, "Your high-pitched snore sounds like music."

Who says that?

I smile from deep inside.

Only my lady would say that my snore sounds like music.

27
Javi

Mɪɴᴜᴛᴇs ᴀꜰᴛᴇʀ ᴡᴇ sᴛᴀʀᴛ ᴏᴜʀ ᴍᴏʀɴɪɴɢ ᴡᴀʟᴋ, sᴛɪʟʟ ɪɴ ᴏᴜʀ cul-de-sac, I stop and stare down at the cold and rough concrete below me. Despite my tiredness and the pain in my stomach, I take a few more steps. I cough as my chest pounds under Blue Sweater. Seconds later, I throw up.

"It's okay, *mi amore*." Tali gives me a few seconds to catch my breath. "We don't have to walk today. Let's go home."

My energy depleted, I squat to pee. Squatting is much easier than lifting my leg. I then face home. I inhale and cry out because the exhale is painful. Like a sheep, I huddle back to my shepherd for protection. As Tali lifts me up, I smell her fear.

She kisses my forehead and says, "Let's go visit Dr. Noah."

In the waiting room, I shiver as I sit on Tali's lap. She caresses me and, despite the nonstop chattering bird, eases me into an untroubled slumber. I awake as Tali shifts to get up.

"Good morning, Javi," Dr. Noah says in a soft voice as he reaches for me. "What's going on, Tal?"

Tali passes me into his arms. "He's been throwing up for the past three days." Her eyes glisten as her hands clasp tightly to her chest as though in prayer.

"Is he coughing up any blood, or have you noticed any blood in his urine or stool?" Dr. Noah puts me down on a cool shiny table.

"No blood. I'd remember."

I'd remember, too.

Dr. Noah pats my head. "He's down two pounds. I'd like to run some blood tests."

Tali nods.

Dr. Noah inserts a needle into my paw and says, "Sorry, Javi."

It's okay. It doesn't hurt.

I watch my blood fill one tube and then another.

Dr. Noah says, "Take Javi home to rest. I'll call you in a few hours."

At home, Tali grabs a pen and paper before she picks up the phone and says, "Hello?" She writes down some stuff. She's not smiling, but she's not crying. "Thank you, Dr. Noah. We'll see you tomorrow morning."

"Well, little man, your blood work is mostly normal."

Hooray.

"Dr. Noah scheduled us for an abdominal ultrasound."

I love how you say us, like you're getting one, too.

"Don't worry, it's noninvasive."

Noninvasive sounds like a scary word. I may have to pretend to be a superhero.

"You can't eat after 8:00 p.m. Food in the stomach makes it harder for the ultrasound to penetrate to the organs."

Penetrate the organs?

After another restless night, I expect the same morning routine: Tali goes to the bathroom and gets dressed, that part stays the same, and then it's my turn. I always have a turn.

"I'm sorry, Javi. No food or water, and you can't pee."

What? Even a superhero has to pee first thing in the morning.

"Dr. Noah wants you to have a full bladder."

I do have a full bladder. That's why I have to pee.

Next thing I know, we're back in the car, and I'm soon back in Dr. Noah's arms. "Let's go, Javi. The ultrasound is fast."

Dr. Noah puts me on a soft bed where a nurse shaves my belly.

Why in the world am I getting a haircut now?

She squeezes warm jelly on my belly and rolls a toy over it again and again.

It tickles. If I didn't have to pee so badly, this would be fun.

Soon enough, the jelly's wiped off my belly. I'm led outside to pee, and then I'm back in the office sitting on Tali's lap.

"It's not good, Tali," Dr. Noah says.

"Tell me." Tali pretends to be strong.

"It looks like a mass by his pyloric sphincter. This is where the stomach meets the duodenum of the small intestines. I suggest an exploratory. And, of course, we'd like to remove the mass."

"When?"

"I've already checked with the surgeon. He can do it today."

Tali's voice shakes. "Let's do whatever needs to be done."

"Tali?" Dr. Noah whispers.

"Yes?" A layer of tears settles on her lower eyelashes.

"You're a great doggy mommy." He smiles first with his eyes and then with his mouth.

My lady nods. There's nothing to say. She runs her tongue over the tear that dripped from her eye, down her cheek, and onto her upper lip. She tucks her chin to the top of my head, swaddles me in our invisible blanket, and, like she's done a million times before, kisses me.

28
Javi

RECUPERATING AT HOME, I LEARN TO ACCEPT THE THINGS I cannot change. For example, I'm tired. Not the kind of tired I can just sleep off but the kind of tired where I lose track of days.

One day, while the sun is coming up, Tali tells me about a dream she had. "Javi, in my dream, you introduced me to a white puppy with black spots named, Binah. You told me that her name means understanding in Hebrew. We both wanted understanding."

Hours later, Tali kisses my head and introduces me to a white puppy with black spots. "Javi, this is your baby sister, Binah."

Binah is a two-month-old Havanese. She's the size of an eight-pound loaf of bread. Her white silky hair rests against her slender body while gentle curls cover her underbelly. Her black velvety ears frame her face, and her tail is a feather of soft white fur. She has a slight fold in her chin, like a dimple on a human, and shows her Chiclet teeth when she smiles, which is often. She's a character, a real joker. In an instant, I love her. Although I feel insecure because of my missing teeth, I feel handsome because Tali had brushed my hair and put on my tie.

Binah makes me feel younger and stronger. In the days that follow, I play mentor. I explain to Binah some house rules.

"There's a list of things you must never do," I tell her. "Number one: Never pee or poop in the house."

"But what if it's raining outside?"

"Never."

Binah nods.

"Number two: Never tear into the indoor or outdoor trash."

"But what if the bag falls open on the floor and displays all of the uneaten leftovers?"

"Never. Rotting garbage is never leftovers."

Binah nods in disgust.

"Number three: Never try on Tali's shoes, especially with your mouth."

"Makes sense. I've got nothing."

"Number four: Never roll over on anything that's dead or near dead. This includes the fish in the pond, worms, squirrels, birds, and bunnies."

"But what if it's my birthday?"

"No. Number five: Never take food from anywhere except from the floor or your bowl on the floor."

Binah's eyes open wide.

I interrupt her thoughts. "Never."

She scrunches up her face like she just swallowed a lemon.

"Finally," I say, "I've got to teach you puppy eyes because . . ."

Binah tilts her head down as her soft eyes gaze upward. She looks like she's about to cry as she whispers, "Please!"

"Jeez, Binah, that's fantastic."

Binah is smart and happy. She'll look you in the eyes as she searches for the answers to her two most important questions: Where's the food? and will you throw the ball?

One morning, it's hailing the size of peas. Before going to work, Tali shoves her feet into her furry boots.

"If you're not too busy, Javi, you're welcome to join us outside."

I consider it for a moment.

No thank you.

I jump up onto the couch and put my nose right up against the window. From the comfort of home, I watch the sunrise over the sleeping houses as Binah crunches through the fresh snow to find a good place to squat. Tali cleans off her car and then shovels the driveway with precision, straight lines and even edges. All the while she waves to me and throws the ball for Binah.

Minutes after the neighborhood slowly wakes up, Tali stamps the snow off her boots and wipes Binah's paws. Inside she takes off her coat, takes off Binah's sweater, and asks cheerfully, "Who's hungry?"

After breakfast, Tali slips me into Blue Sweater and Binah back into Pink Sweater, and we all go out into the backyard. There is peace in the untouched fallen snow and the undisturbed pond. Tali blows warm breath into her hands before she paves a path for

137

me to pee and throws the ball for Binah, who runs wildly, creating a zigzag path. She stops now and then to shake off the big flakes that stick to her eyelashes.

After Tali goes to work, Binah and I snuggle on the couch to watch cartoons on TV. *Superman* is our favorite show.

Binah asks me, "What makes a superhero?"

"Well, Binah, superheroes have a special power. They're committed to helping others. They usually fight villains, and sometimes, they wear capes.

"Can a dog be a superhero?"

"Sure. Why not?"

"Even though you wear a blue sweater instead of a cape, I think you're a superhero, Javi."

"Thank you, Binah."

"Do you think I can be a superhero one day?"

"Absolutely! You can be Super Binah."

We sleep next to each other until the key turns in the door.

"Mommy's home," Binah barks as she races to greet Tali.

On our short walk, I stay close to Tali and move the slowest as Binah ventures as far as she can on her leash. She rarely chooses to walk the clear and well-traveled path. She prefers a road more likely to have the foul-smelling smorgasbord of rotting leaves and disintegrating carcasses, even if this means getting a pine needle stuck in her paw. This happened twice so far.

"Hey, Javi, do you smell what I smell?"

"My nose isn't what it used to be. These days it's more like an ornament on my face. Whaddaya smell?"

"I smell bacon."

"Are you sure? I think I'd smell bacon."

"I'm certain I smell bacon. It's getting closer."

My eyesight isn't much better than my sense of smell, but my instinct is clearer than ever. I know how this will end; I, too, had my bloopers.

"BACON!" Binah barks with confidence.

"Binah, hold on. Slow down." I try to catch up despite four of my strides equaling one of hers. I've never seen any dog move this fast. I call out, "I wouldn't get any closer if I were you."

Three seconds.

"I LOVE bacon."

Two seconds.

"I'm just saying as your older brother who knows."

One second.

"Hello, Bacon." She plunges into the poop and bathes herself in it until Tali's voice catches up to her brain.

"NO! NO! NO!"

Binah's disappointed. Of course, she wants to enjoy the experience a bit longer.

"Hey, Javi, do you want to hear a dirty joke?"

I smile. "I'm looking at one."

Binah laughs. "What do dogs call frozen poop?"

"What?" I bark, egging her, on although I know the answer.

"Poopsicles," she barks.

Back home, Tali introduces Binah to bath time. "How in the world do you manage to get so dirty?"

"Well, Mommy, I'm a lot closer to the ground than you are."

As her stink funnels its way down the drain, Binah cries out, "I want to smell like bacon."

One dog's waste is another dog's treasure.

29
Binah

"HEY GUYS, DO YOU MIND IF I STOP HERE FOR A SECOND?"

Daisy: "No."

Cooper: "Nope."

Chloe: "Not at all."

Me: "I remember this so clearly. For thirty seconds I was in bacon-poop heaven. For thirty minutes I was literally in hot water. I love that Javi remembered this. It's so interesting to hear the story from his point of view."

Cooper: "How come Javi called your mommy *Tali*?"

Chloe: Weren't you paying attention?"

Cooper: "What? What'd I miss?"

Daisy: "Javi had a mommy before Tali and a mama before that. You can only have one of each."

Me: "That's not true. You can have more than one mom or dad. Elvis had two dads."

Cooper: "Can you please get back to Javi's story?"

Me: "Javi laughed so hard that day. At first, I thought he was choking because it sounded like a cough."

Cooper cannonballed into the far end of the pond. "Get to the point." He climbed out of the water, onto the rocks, and shook out his hair like, you know, a dog.

Me: "I got scared when Javi couldn't catch his breath. I knew he wasn't feeling well, but seconds later, it became a long period of giggling. Finally, it turned into one uncontrollable laugh that escaped out into the hallway and made Mommy run in from wherever she was. In less than three seconds, Mommy was tickling both of us, and we were all laughing."

I miss you, Javi. You're still my favorite superhero.

My three best friends, Daisy, Chloe, and Cooper, laughed until the daylight disappeared, and everyone went home. Mommy sat by the picturesque pond with her book opened and her eyes closed.

In the dusk, the pond was lit by spotlights underneath the water that made the fish look like battery-operated toys. I focused on my favorite past time: my ball-ball. I dropped it into the water, hoping one of the fish would toss it back out to me. In the end, it was Mommy who got the ball-ball out from the pond and threw it across the yard one last time before we went into the house.

30
Javi

I TELL BINAH, "DISCIPLINE. THAT'S WHAT YOU NEED."

"Is discipline something Mommy can buy for me?"

"No, it's not."

"Is discipline something you can do for me?"

"No, it's not."

"Uh-oh. How am I going to get it?"

"You're going to practice it. Discipline is self-control. It's the decision to wait for something, like a treat, rather than get it or take it right away."

"That sounds hard."

"It sounds hard because it is hard. Habits are part of our nature. Changing our habits will be uncomfortable at first."

"Uncomfortable like having a pine needle stuck in my paw?"

"Not exactly. Pretend your world is the size of your bed."

"Oh, now you're talking. My bed is very comfortable."

"Exactly, but pretend that anything outside of your bed, like big dogs and doctors, are scary and, therefore, uncomfortable."

Binah's eyes widen. "Big dogs and doctors *are* scary. So is going up and down the steps."

"Yes, big dogs and doctors are scary now because you haven't met a sweet big dog like my friend Elvis or a caring doctor like Dr. Noah. And the steps are only scary for you now because you haven't learned how to climb them yet."

"Did you climb the steps when you were younger, Javi?"

"Yes, I did. But at first I was afraid of steps. Every day, I practiced climbing them, and the more I practiced, the easier they were to climb."

"I'm still afraid of steps."

"Binah, the only way you learn to not be afraid of something is to travel outside of your comfort zone. Do you understand?"

"I understand. New behaviors are uncomfortable only until, with enough practice, they become habits that are comfortable."

"Very good, Binah. And choose healthy behaviors so that you develop healthy habits."

"Javi, what's the worst habit you've ever had?"

"My worst habit was listening to and sometimes believing the negative voice in my head. I learned that our negative voice can wake up melon collie, who then can steal our joy. I also learned that I can stop this negative voice."

"WHAT? You can? Javi, you're a superhero."

"You can stop the negative voice, too, Binah."

"How?"

"Be compassionate. Our negative voices don't make us bad dogs. As Tali will tell you over and over again, you're a good dog. But, sometimes we want immediate comfort." I look into Binah's eyes. "I learned that my negative voice feeds off my vulnerability. If I'm tired, hungry, or sad, that voice takes advantage. I have to be really strong to win this fight. Do you understand?"

"I understand, Javi. Our negative voice is the villain. We have to use our positive voice to rise above our negative voice. We may struggle, but in the end, we're going to win because we're the superheroes."

31
Javi

AFTER LIVING WITH TALI FOR THREE YEARS, I HAVE GOTTEN comfortable with my daily rituals: walk, eat, nap, find cookies, nap again, and look out the window for any moving object, whether it's a passing dog, human, car, bunny, squirrel, bug, or leaf. When Tali returns home from work, we'd walk again, eat again, and then we'd go down for our longest nap. I have my preferences about where I eat and sleep, and I noticed that Tali has preferences, too. She watches the news while she eats breakfast, listens to music while she reads, and sings a prayer to me before bed.

I love that Little Miss Binah changed all that. Now, in the morning Tali takes us both for a short walk, brings me home, and takes Binah out for a longer walk. She feeds us the same delicious, homemade breakfast. I love lapping up the egg's delicious yellow liquid that flows out beneath the cheese. How long my morning naps last depends on how much energy Binah has. The game

Peekaboo easily replaces my naps. Make sacrifices. That's what big brothers do, right?

I tell Binah, "Peekaboo supports how important eye contact is. Without it, there's no game."

"Am I smart enough to play?"

"Of course, Binah. All you have to do is cover your eyes."

"Like this, Javi?"

"Perfect, Binah. Do you notice that, even with your eyes covered, you're still able to see me in your mind?"

"Yes, Javi. I can still see you in my mind."

"That's because you're smart. You're smart enough to still see me when you don't see me and smart enough to take care of Mommy when I'm actually gone."

I know that Binah's too young to understand the Rainbow Bridge, but I still have to prepare her.

"Gone? Where ya going, Javi?"

"I'm going over the Rainbow Bridge."

"Can I go with you?"

"Definitely not. You have to take care of Mommy."

"For how long?"

"I don't know, Binah, but I'll be back."

When Tali's key turns in the door, it's Binah who greets her first.

"Mommy's home! Mommy's home! Yayayayayayay!"

We all take another short walk. I take the fastest route to the sidewalk and quickly pee, fully committed to emptying my bladder. My days of holding back to mark territory are gone. Tali then takes me home, and I wait for them to return from their longer walk. We eat Tali's home-cooked dinner of salmon or chicken with rice and carrots and go outside in the backyard to pee. It's the month of May, the right season to teach Binah about the three heavenly bodies of the dandelion.

"The yellow flower implies the sun, the puff ball resembles the moon, and the seeds look like the stars. Close your eyes, make a wish, and blow, blow, blow like the wind."

My wish is always the same.

"What did you wish for, Javi?"

"I wished to come back as a little boy."

"A human?"

"Yes, Binah, a human."

"Wow!" Binah closes her eyes, makes her wish, and blows the seeds into the air.

Before bed, Tali sings the bedtime prayer to us. I sleep on one side of Tali while Binah sleeps on the other side.

Binah whispers, "Knock, knock."

I ask, "Who's there?"

"Atch."

"Atch who?"

"God bless you, my brother, Javi." She rolls over laughing. "Get it? Atch who? Achoo. Ah choo."

Yes, Little Miss Binah changed everything, but it was all for the better.

32
Javi

Now eleven and a half years old, I prefer standing to walking, lying to standing, and sleeping to any of the above. Although my hearing is decent, I have difficulty seeing at night and no longer rely on my sense of smell. I've lost the desire to explore, and I've stopped reading and answering the neighborhood pee mail. However, I still get excited to see my best friend. Whenever Binah hangs out with Daisy, Chloe, or Cooper, Tali invites Misty over for a date with me.

"Misty, you look marvelous!" I bark.

"Some days I look in the mirror and like what I see—other days, not so much."

"When you look in the mirror, your gorgeous green eyes see only half of you, but I see all of you. Trust me, you're awesome."

"Thank you, Javi. You can't spell awesome without me."

We both laugh.

She's right.

We talk about the past, how we miss Elvis and Ali. We complain about the present, stiffness in our joints and gum disease. Misty tells me about her failing kidneys, and I tell her about my cancer. We wonder about the future: Will we remember our greatest joys and dreams? We both agree that the things we remember best are the things that we repeat over and over until we remember that we've remembered them.

Misty smirks. "What's your strangest human story?"

I half smile and say, "I don't want to be disrespectful."

"They talk about us all the time," Misty laughs. "Besides, we're old. Their stories will die with us."

"Okay. I remember watching a tennis game on TV with my dad, Roger. Every time his favorite tennis player, whose name was also Roger, won, my dad shouted, 'We won!'"

Misty giggles. "That's definitely a human thing."

"But we didn't win. Roger, the tennis player, won. We watched. From the comfort of our home, we watched."

"Javi, whaddaya trying to say?"

"It's the same with life. If we want to win in our lives, then we can't sit still. We have to play."

"We did play, Javi. We played a good game." Misty kisses me and places her paw on the small of my back.

I feel a jolt of electricity race through my body. She still gives me goose bumps.

Misty says, "My dad doesn't know how to fix anything around the house, but, boy oh boy, does he try."

"I bet your dad put the thingamajig inside the doohickey, turned the whatchamacallit, and whateveritwas still didn't work."

Misty snorts. "Doodad, thingy, gizmo, thingwhatnot."

We laugh so hard that we each pee a little.

I've loved Misty from the moment that I met her. I feel the same way about Tali. That's just the way life is sometimes.

That night, like most nights, I lay with Allie Gator at the foot of Tali's bed while Binah rests at the top of the bed.

That's when I notice it. Binah has her own birthmark.

"Hey, Binah!"

She picks up her head. "Yeah?"

I open my mouth, stick out my tongue, show her my birthmark and say, "Unlike my heart, hidden on my tongue, your permanent heart is displayed on the outside of your body for all to see."

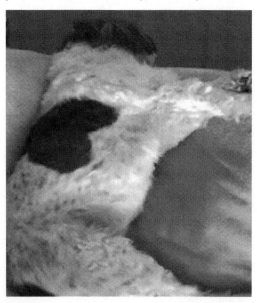

Can you see it?

Tali whispers, "Javi."

I sit up and wag my tail.

"You are a very good boy." She smiles reassuringly. "Come here, *mi amore*."

I curl up into her empty arm. I'm happy to be a very good boy—her *mi amore*. This is my calming thought before my ears fill with Tali singing the familiar bedtime prayer, and I slip into a quick and exhausted sleep.

33
Javi

I<small>T'S A WARM NIGHT IN JUNE. BINAH AND I SIT ON THE PAVERS BY</small> the pond while the sun sets. I nod in the direction of Daisy's house.

I say to Binah, "Always love Daisy. Friends are so important. They make you less vulnerable to melon collie."

"I promise to always love Daisy and Chloe and Cooper."

"Be your true self and not some imitation of someone else. And remember what you do for only yourself will die with you. What you do for others will live on much longer."

"Thanks for the pup talk, Javi. I will remember all of that."

In the twilight, Binah becomes frozen in time: her fur is as white as milk. Her black velvety ears frame her face, and her lips, slightly parted, display her Chiclet teeth.

"My mind's playing tricks on me," I say out loud. Everything is out of focus. I'm confused as to who's in front of me—Binah? I think it's Princess Leia. "I miss you," I try to shout, feeling distant from my voice. I think it's Binah who says something, but I can't hear her. I'm too far away. Mama appears, but in a matter of seconds, all of her fades away. I cry out, "I miss my baby sister."

"Javi? Javi!" a paw gently touches my face.

Princess Leia?

"Snap out of it, Javi. How many fingers do you see?"

Binah?

I try to focus.

Binah's joking. She doesn't have any fingers.

I try to sit up, but I sink back down into the grass.

Princess Leia sits down next to me. I can tell that she's nervous by the way her ears drop and her tail wilts.

"Javi?" Binah whimpers.

The back door opens, and cool air rushes out from the inside.

"Mommy, Mommy," Binah cries out. "Javi needs help."

As I cough up thick, rust-colored phlegm, I see little bursts of blinding light. Silver stars explode like it's Independence Day.

Tali's muffled voice sounds far away. In the past, to get her attention, I'd usually get close to her, make an obvious noise, look her in the eyes, and then push my wet nose on her lap. Now, there's no time for that.

"JAVI!" Tali scoops me up into her arms and hurries me outside the backyard gate. Binah, left behind, uses her paws to give her side of the fence a tough workout. I hear her heartbreaking howl.

That's the last thing I remember about that day.

When I wake up, I smell Tali's fear, hear her sniffling, and feel her rapid heartbeat. In between the thumps, I see her bite her lip.

That's the last thing I remember about that day.

I wake up and recognize his scent, his voice, and his gentle touch.

Dr. Noah says, "I called Mommy this morning, Javi."

I love how you speak to me like I'm a little human.

"I'm not enthusiastic about her visiting you this morning."

Enthusiastic is a big word, but I know what it means.

I'm not enthusiastic to hear you say that.

"You need rest. You get too excited when Mommy's here."

I love to hear you call Tali mommy. That's her name. Mommy.

"I told her that sometimes there is a turn for the worse several days after surgery. I told her that you were iffy."

Iffy? That's a new word. I don't know what it means.

"You're struggling, Javi."

Oh. Okay. I'm struggling.

I hope Princess Leia didn't struggle. I like thinking about Princess Leia.

My mind drifts. I'm warm, and I'm cold. I watch the light until my eyes grow heavy.

My heart can't take the beating.

That's the last thing I remember about that day.

34
Binah

OH MY GOD, THIS IS SO HARD TO READ.

Nobody thinks the way Javi did. Nobody shares his vision. He wanted to have an impact on the world, to teach humans to see the world differently, perhaps a bit more lovingly. He was 100 percent committed to pursuing his dream. He was brave enough to believe that he could transform from the dog he was into the little human he wanted to become.

Daisy: "Was Javi ever blessed by Saint Francis?"

I heard Daisy, but I wasn't ready to answer her question. I licked my paws to calm myself down. My friends didn't understand my sadness. How could they? They didn't lose a brother like Javi.

Daisy: "Binah?"

Me: "Who's Saint Francis?"

Daisy: "He was a man who loved animals. Every year on the first Sunday in October, in his memory, churches welcome pets for a prayer and a sprinkle of holy water. It's a special ceremony called the Blessing of the Animals."

Me: I don't know. I wasn't around in October. I arrived in April and Javi passed in July.

The conversation ended when Cooper and his mom, Carol, came through the backyard gate. Carol quickly let Cooper off leash, and he sprinted toward us. Unable to brake in time, he landed in the pond.

Carol called out, "Cooper, what did I tell you? Behave!"

We all laughed. I was happy to be laughing with my friends.

Mommy, Phyllis, and Marissa were talking as they ate and drank on the deck. I watched Carol give Mommy a bag. I knew from Mommy's smile and her eye contact with me that it wasn't human food. It's got to be treats for me and my friends.

"Snack time," Mommy called out.

I was the leader, the first to leap onto the deck. I don't know who was second, third, or fourth, but Carol was in charge.

"Hi, Carol. May I call you Carol?" I barked as I gave her my paw.

Carol wore sunglasses above her smile. Her voice was happy. "Binah, you're such a good girl." She held a treat in her hand. I took my treat and went to the back of the line, hoping that she would forget that I was first in line and give me another treat.

Daisy, Chloe, and Cooper got their treats and were back to running around. I lingered on the deck.

What can I say? I love my treats.

"Hi, Carol. May I call you Carol?" I barked a second time with my chin pressed on her thigh. I tried my best to look angelic.

"Binah, you're such a good girl," Carol laughed and gave me another treat.

For a few brief moments, I was really happy.

35
Javi

"HI, JAVI. IT'S DR. NOAH."

I think that's such a polite thing to do, say hi and introduce yourself, especially since I'm not a little human yet.

I watch his mouth move. He whispers, "How are you feeling, little guy? You shouldn't be in any pain."

No pain.

"You're a good boy, Javi. We'll keep you comfortable."

I can't lift my head. The film on my eyes makes everything blurry. I allow my eyes to close until I smell Tali's stress hormones, and then I open my eyes a fraction.

My lady. Mommy!

Despite the head cone, Mommy finds a way to hold me. Her voice cracks. "You're healing nicely, *mi amore*." She holds me until I fall asleep. I'm sure she held me for hours while I slept.

I don't remember.

I see Mama. She tells me, "Endings are new beginnings."

When I wake up I'm alone. I cry out, "Mommy!"

"Hi, Javi." A tear drips from Dr. Noah's eye. Or maybe it's from my medicine drip. He covers me with a blanket and moves a tiny pillow closer to me. The pillow has a rainbow.

Can this be the Rainbow Bridge?

Dr. Noah gently pats my head. "Rest, Javi. Mommy will be here soon."

While I rest, the Jo- Jo- Jonah song plays over and over again in my head until I hear Dr. Noah's and Tali's voices. He tells her a bunch of sentences.

Something. Something. Something.

I imagine that Tali stops breathing for a few seconds. She needs more time for the words to travel to her brain.

She whispers, "I'm so sorry, *mi amore*. If only I could help." She kisses my head and puts her hands together in a praying position. She doesn't try to hide the lines around her mouth that deepen as she tightens her lips.

36
Binah

WHEN MOMMY STARTED WORKING A THIRD JOB THREE NIGHTS a week, Marissa and Bill looked after me. I think all this work helped Mommy to ignore melon collie. To reciprocate, Daisy stayed with us two mornings a week. One day, after breakfast, Daisy peed behind the treadmill and had the nerve to act as if it was no big deal.

My negative voice roared, "Daisy, what's wrong with you?"

"What'd I do now? Why are you yelling at me?"

"I hate when you pee in my house. It makes my mommy sad and she's already sad that Javi's gone."

"That's why I peed behind the treadmill. She won't see it."

That made me roar louder. "You're a poopy head. I don't like you anymore."

Daisy cried.

Mommy came downstairs with wet hair and wet eyes. "Girls, are you ready to go to the park?"

Daisy barked, "Yes."

I barked louder. "No."

At the park, I no longer had the oomph to run and play. Instead, I dug at the ball-ball with my paws, touching it, but failing to dislodge it from the low branches of the bush.

DOES ANYONE ELSE CARE ABOUT THIS BALL-BALL?

With one eye, I watched Daisy and her short legs drag a big stick. With the other eye, I watched Chloe scratch her tail and Cooper prance around with a sock hanging so low from his mouth that it nearly touched the ground. Within seconds, Daisy dropped the stick by Cooper's front paws, collapsed, rolled over on her back and passively let Cooper sniff her all over.

She makes me sick.

Mommy said goodbye to Phyllis and Carol, and Chloe and Cooper said goodbye to Daisy and me. The three of us, Mommy, Daisy and I, then walked in silence back to Daisy's house. Mommy turned the key to open the door. "Daisy, your mommy will be home soon. We love you."

I barked, "Speak for yourself, Mommy."

Daisy whimpered, "I said I was sorry, Binah. I love you."

I barked back, "You still don't understand. Love is an action word. You show love by giving, not by deceiving."

Back in the comfort of my backyard, and in the discomfort of my mind, I felt a whimper build as something stirred inside of me. I growled as the hair on the back of my neck instantly rose. Although my negative voice was silent, hopelessness glared from my eyes. With melon collie wide awake, peace had deserted me.

I wandered aimlessly in the backyard until I spotted my ghostly reflection in the pond. I held out my paw to the fish. In less than a blink of an eye, I fell into the water.

Mommy must've flown out of the kitchen window to scoop me up. The muck from the pond made me as slippery as a wet bar of soap. I shook myself from head to tail, ridding myself of most of the yucky pond water. I stretched my paws up as high as I could on Mommy's legs until she lifted me up again. I could feel the anguish of melon collie, the anguish in me.

I felt my negativity twist my mouth and turn my eyes cockeyed before growling, "I'm afraid."

"It's okay, Binah." Mommy tried to comfort me.

I struggled with my thoughts.

Knock, knock.

I whispered, "Is that you knocking, Javi?"

Yes. Choose your positive voice over your negative voice.

I whispered again, "I think melon collie's knocking too. Should I let her in?"

Absolutely not! Let her knock. You don't have to answer. If you let her in, she'll definitely mess up your mind. Melon collie wants nothing more than to steal your joy. Please don't be sad.

"I'm not sad, Javi. I just really miss you. I like hearing your reassuring voice in my head."

This is your voice, Binah. Whatever you focus on is what you bring to your experience. Don't waste your energy focusing on the negative, what you don't want. Let that go. Instead, use your energy to focus on the positive, what you do want. You'll see. Energy flows where your attention goes.

I whimpered, "Javi, since you're gone, my negative thoughts have become more habitual."

That's the fear talking. Don't allow your negative voice to hold you hostage and activate melon collie. Shake off the negativity.

I shouted, "GO AWAY, MELON COLLIE, NOBODY'S HOME!"

I wiggled until Mommy put me back down. I had everything I wanted to say worked out perfectly in my head, but as soon as I barked it was as if my negative voice had scrambled my words into something ridiculous. I took a deep breath and started over.

"You listen to me, melon collie." I was no longer afraid to address her by name. "I want you to know that I recognize your negative voice. You're nothing but a bully. One day, I won't be scared of you. I'll destroy you—not the way you try to destroy me with fear and sadness, but instead with kindness and compassion, just like my brother Javi taught me. I'll destroy you with love."

Good job, Binah. How do you feel?

"I feel much better, Javi. Thank you."

Then I feel better, too. When one of us is well, we are both well because we are one.

That night, I struggled to sleep. I felt like I had disappointed Javi. He wouldn't want me to be angry at Daisy. I imagined another conversation:

Javi: "Daisy's actions and reactions are not about you, Binah. They're about her."

Me: "I wish I could forgive her."

Javi: "Turn 'I wish' into 'I will.'"

Me: "I can't."

Javi: "Turn 'I can't' into 'I can.'"

Me: "How?"

Javi: "Change the way you think. What if Daisy is in your life to help you change for the better? What if she's a messenger sent to remind you to be patient? It's the negative voice inside of *you*, not Daisy, who prevents you from being your best self. I prescribe a heaping tablespoon of love, understanding, and patience for both of you."

I took a deep breath.

Javi: "What upsets you about Daisy serves as a reminder to what you need to work on yourself. Change yourself, and those around you will change."

That was the end of my internal dialogue.

I knew I needed to apologize to Daisy.

The next morning, I found a peace offering at our back door. It was Daisy's favorite cookie. She'd have brought me a bunny if she was fast enough to catch one.

We never fought again.

37
Javi

Endless darkness spins around me until I feel a "knock-knock" on my head. I think it's Binah telling a joke.

Who's there?

"It's the Light," says the Light.

Another voice boomerangs in my head.

"All done," says Dr. Noah. "He's not in any pain."

My blood feels warm.

My fate as a dog was always for humans to decide. As a human, I'll choose my own fate plus the fate of my dog.

Mommy smells sad. "Go home, *mi amore*."

Where's Binah? She didn't finish her knock-knock joke.

"You're not going to be sick anymore."

Neha?

"He looks so peaceful."

Roger?

"I'll leave the four of you alone," says Dr. Noah.

The circle of Mommy, Neha, and Roger grew smaller, like a closing umbrella.

Wow. You're all here together—for me.

"It will be less than one minute before he stops breathing."

I'm still breathing? Tell me what to do.

"Walk with me," says Praying Mantis.

Who are you?

"I am the Land Lord," says Praying Mantis.

What do you want with me?

"I am here to take you home," says Praying Mantis.

Home? I don't understand.

I'm driving Silver Car from Oz's Matchbox collection. Princess Leia is in the back seat. Praying Mantis sits in the front passenger seat. I avoid several obstacles on the road. Even though I can no longer see, I remain calm for my sister.

That's what big brothers do.

I say, "Princess Leia, would you please remove my blindfold?"

She says, "You're not wearing one, Javi."

"Let go of the wheel," coaches Praying Mantis.

Although I'm afraid, I listen and let go of the wheel.

"Tap on the brake," instructs Praying Mantis.

After I tap on the brake, we safely stop by a river.

Mommy says, "Look at the water, *mi amore.*"

Silver Car turns into Silver Boat. Princess Leia waves goodbye.

Mommy sings as the boat floats up the river. "Row, row, row

your boat, gently down the stream. Merrily, merrily, merrily, merrily, life is but a dream."

"You're the captain of your own ship," says Roger.

I'm the captain!

"Feel the waves, *mi amore*." I feel Mommy's gentle touch. "Look for where the water meets the sky, and you'll see the beautiful rainbow. Go to the brilliant, magnificent Light, Javi. Go."

"Come," says the Light. "Do not look back."

A thin beam of light spills through a crack in the universe.

Mommy says, "Go, Javi. It's okay. Go with the Light."

"Follow me to the Light," says Praying Mantis.

I'm going, Mommy.

Mommy gasps for air. "You're my superhero, Javi."

"The spirit controls the mind, and the mind controls the body," says the Light. "Let go."

I'm a superhero!

"Come," repeats the Light.

I still hear Mommy. She says, "Follow the Light, *mi amore*."

Like a good boy, I follow the Light. I feel lighter and wide awake. I'm lifted up, soaring to new heights. My long hair blows in the wind like the dispersing seeds of a dandelion. With endless energy, I dance, and spin, and run, and race, and fly, and soar across a bridge toward the Light.

Goodbye, Mommy. I love you. I'll see you again someday. Goodbye, Neha and Roger. I love you, too.

38
Binah

I'M SAD. IT JUST BECAME CLEAR TO ME THAT JAVI GOT A ONE-WAY ticket over the Rainbow Bridge. I thought that he was coming back home.

Did he know he wasn't coming back?

It no longer mattered that I, too, had wished for Javi to come back as a little boy before I blew, blew, blew like the wind. That was last May, when Javi taught me about the three heavenly bodies of the dandelion. None of this mattered anymore.

With zero enthusiasm I paced the house. Upstairs, downstairs, and then back upstairs again. I refused to look out of my favorite living room window where I had sat for hours, day after day, looking for signs that Javi was coming home. I wondered what happened to him.

I missed Javi. I loved him. I'd always love him no matter what.

39
Javi

A SURGE OF ENERGY PULLS ME UPWARD LIKE A MAGNET. I SLIP
out of my body as if I had slipped out of Blue Sweater. I see my
lifeless younger body. My thoughts and actions happen in both
slow motion and at rapid speed. I hear a rushing sound.

Whoosh.

I slide up a vortex of Light. I swirl feet first like I'm going
down a slide, but again, I'm going up. I see Mama.

Hi, Mama!

I feel a pang of longing.

"You finished your mission," Mama says.

What does that mean?

"You served others. Your spirit has grown. You're ready."

Ready for what?

"You must let go."

Again?

"We're only here for a short while. You can't stay here."

Where am I going?

"Destiny."

I think I understand.

"Bye for now, my son."

Goodbye Mama. I'll see you again.

Mama reminds me, "Look in front of you. Don't look back."

But I do look back. My brain plays movies in my head. I watch as a series of events unfold. The volume is off. Mama's feeding me, and I'm feeding Princess Leia; Roger's holding me with one hand, and Neha's holding me with two hands. Sarai's loose curls dangle over my face as she laughs, and I kiss Oz as he cries.

This is neither in color nor in black and white.

I play wrestle with Elvis, chase after beautiful Misty, box with Ali, snuggle with Tali, and catch a glimpse of Pinocchio.

Sepia. That's the color.

Finally, I introduce Binah to the dandelions. I teach her to blow, blow, blow like the wind. I am calm. The movie ends.

Speaking of movies, I search unsuccessfully for Pinocchio dressed in boy clothes. I had hoped to hear his words of wisdom, lessons he learned from his transformation. I wanted to be convinced that there truly was a creator.

I feel the warmth of the sun. I see the puffy moon, and I reach for the stars. Close up, the stars are brightly illuminated, not like the faint glow that Oz and Sarai saw from the thingamajig. My long tail wags exponentially fast as I run across the multicolored bridge surrounded by multicolored clouds. I'm unfamiliar with so much color. So many new shades that I've never seen before. I actually experience the colors. I feel them. I become a part of them. Without saying a word, I hear my soul speak.

Hi, my name is Javi. I'm here to see my creator.

I hear God speak to me. "Javi, your existence in this world is not an accident. I, the creator of the universe, the sun, the moon, and the stars, and the creator of all the humans and animals that have ever lived, purposely created you."

Me?

"I see everything that occurs. Secrets are not hidden from me. I know your innermost thoughts and dreams. Many of our limitations are more perceived than real. Often, it's only phantoms, like a negative voice or melon collie, that hold us back. But nothing holds you back now, Javi. You are free."

Free?

"Javi, my boy, you have done exceedingly well. Without love we are nothing. You made humans love. You challenged yourself and others to come face-to-face with their own negativity. You learned many important lessons: it's easy to love when you love, but hard to love when you hate. When you believe someone can change, they do. Everyone has a spark of Light and, therefore, can be forgiven."

I'm listening, God.

"You understand that dreams are to be pursued at all costs. The bigger the obstacles, the more meaningful the journey and the greater the glory."

Yes. I absolutely understand.

"You will travel to the next level. It's another universe beyond these majestic mountains, with both positive and negative energies. Do not adopt either, or you will become mindless. You will be tested to overcome human desires."

I become weightless as I float into a spectacular darkness of endless nothingness. And although it's nothing, at the same time it's everything. I'm now a part of nothing and everything that is Light and love. My head whizzes around and around.

I can't believe how gigantic this place is.

"You learned the biggest secrets are concealed in the unknown and miracles cannot happen in your comfort zone. No more fear. Be brave. This is the ultimate letting go."

Auras of musical light surround water that flows upward and sideways. I see where the water meets the sky, and I see the brilliant, magnificent Light. I become the music and a vibration effortlessly somersaulting inside of it. My thoughts become my actions.

"You are loved."

I am everything.

"Javi, you are a part of me. Your name is my name."

I am now a part of You?

"You were, are, and always will be a part of me."

Was I a good boy?

"You were, are, and always will be a good boy."

What about when I rolled around in poop?

Being curious is part of being alive. You passed your tests."

Just like when I passed the test to be a pet therapist?

"Yes. Your mistakes were, are, and always will be for your soul's lessons. Mistakes help you to climb to a higher level."

What level am I at right now?

"What level do you want to be at?"

I want to be at a human level.

"Then be."

The magnificent voice disappears.

40
Binah

JAVI SENT THAT CHAPTER TO ME IN A DREAM. I BELIEVE EVERY word because I've never heard anything like that before. Javi was super strong, a true superhero.

Daisy and I were besties again. We stuck together like peanut butter and jelly. We walked side by side in front of Mommy, confirming our friendship, even though days before I had declared war, and seconds before we each had claimed ownership of the same stick. We reached Starbarks Park.

Me: "Hey, Cooper."

Cooper: "Hey, Binah. Hi, Daisy. What's up?"

Me: "What are the strongest days of the week?"

Daisy: "I know. I know. Pick me." She performed the hokey pokey in our little circle.

Me: "Daisy, you're adorable. Okay, I pick you."

Daisy: "The weak don't have strong days. They're weak."

Me: "Good try, but the answer is Saturday and Sunday."

Daisy: "What? Why?"

Me: "Because the rest are weekdays."

Daisy: "Huh?"

Me: "Weekdays spelled W-E-A-K days."

Daisy: "I don't get it."

Me: "Not weekdays, W-E-E-K, but W-E-A-K days."

Daisy: "I still don't get it."

Cooper tumbled in the grass and said, "That's a big bug!"

I saw it and felt immediate joy. "That's a praying mantis."

I feel you, Javi. Because of you, I now recognize my negative voice and the sadness that melon collie brings. When I'm calm and the noise in my head is silent, I feel you and I know with certainty that you watch over us from the rainbow.

THE NEW BEGINNING

"The best way to predict the future
is to create it."

—Abraham Lincoln

41
Javi

I WATCH MOMMY TAKE A QUIET CAR RIDE WITH AUNT KIM, WHO occasionally calls out, "Turn left" and "Turn right." Once, she says, "Oops, I think we passed it," and finally, "There it is."

Rainbow Bridge Pet Memorial Park.

The sun warms up the birdbath while the sprinklers cool down the flowers. Pebbled pathways lead to sheds and benches scattered around the large property. I read the little headstones.

Love. Molly. Pluto. Coco. Seamus. Loki. Duke. Bailey.

Aunt Kim looks at her watch and says, "Whenever you're ready, whatever you need, I'm here for you, Tali."

Mommy gently squeezes Aunt Kim's hand before she gets out of the car and walks toward a small building. The rocks crunch beneath her feet. Aunt Kim follows her.

Inside a woman speaks softly. "Hello. My name is Cindy. May I help you?"

"Javi," is all Mommy can say.

Don't cry.

Cindy says, "Please, come with me. I'll take you to Javi."

Aunt Kim hugs Mommy and says, "I'll be right here."

Cindy walks Tali down a gravel road. The uneven turf gives Mommy a limp. They stop at a shed that looks like a little house, similar to the shed in our backyard.

"Take all the time you need," Cindy says as she opens the door. "I'll be in the office if you need anything."

Tali whispers, "Thank you."

The door closes.

This is weird.

I'm as stiff as G.I. Joe, sleeping on a little bed, covered with a little blanket. My head rests on a little pillow. A narrow waterfall of my gray beard lays in between my blond hairs. I smile when I see my missing bottom teeth.

"You look so peaceful, *mi amore.*"

I sniff to smell Mommy, but I smell nothing. Nothing! All my life I've smelled everything, not just coffee, perfume, and cookies baking in the oven. I really miss that one. But I've also smelled love, sadness, and Mommy's unexplainable individual scent. I'm hit with a pang of homesickness. I long for Tali, my mommy, to brush my hair.

Seconds later it hits her. She sees me as I really am—gone.

Oh, how she cries.

With a heavy heart, heavy like it was soaked in concrete and left to dry, Mommy whispers, "Precious Javi. I fell in love. I broke my heart. Now, I have a long road to recovery." She catches her breath, wipes her nose, and scrunches the tissue up before she buries it inside of her fist. "I thought we had more time, much more time. I miss watching you eat from my hand and hearing you sigh when little bits of food fall out of your mouth. I miss listening to you snore while you sleep with your eyes open." She kisses my head. "And I really miss that you smelled liked Cheetos right before you needed a bath." She tries to smile. "You were my best friend, helper, and road trip buddy. You were the best choice I ever made."

She looks under the blanket at my body, scarred from surgery weeks earlier. "Thank you for being my teacher and for giving me so much joy. You are the most precious little dog I've ever met." She exhales slowly. "We'll see one another again." She tries to smooth out the wrinkles around her eyes. "I love you, *mi amore*."

I'm hit with a second wave of longing for the way things used to be. My inability to respond is deafening. Silence is now my dominant character trait. This old soul says nothing. If only Mommy can hear my thoughts.

I love you too, Mommy. I hope you know how much I loved being with you. Thank you for loving me and taking care of me. I haven't given up on my dream. Please don't give up on yours. I will see you again.

Without turning around, Mommy opens the door and steps out into the sunshine. I gasp for fresh air but find none. I no longer feel the warmth of the sun. I feel nothing except for the tugging, the yearning, to somehow start again, this time to accomplish my dream, what I've always wanted—to become a little boy.

Mommy closes the door behind her.

This is when I know my story in this lifetime is over. I say goodbye to my life as I had once known it.

42
Binah

MY DREAMS ARE VIVID, LIKE ACTUAL CONVERSATIONS WITH Javi. This is my sign, the one I'd been waiting for. Javi's okay. Now, I have to pay attention. I'm sure Javi will tell me what to do.

Outside the air felt crisp, the sky was steely blue, and the leaves on the trees had just started to turn yellowish-brown, orange, and red. Although I sniffed at several worms, I didn't eat any, and didn't have nearly enough time to roll around on any before the gang arrived. We played tag.

I was it.

We all learned to tackle, tag, run, and make faces at each other. Our mutual nods initiated the chase. Even panting in quick bursts could be a signal to play. Completely dog-tired, literally, I tagged

Daisy, and we all collapsed on the ground, wagging our tails and tongues, and gazing into each other's eyes.

Me: "What kind of human has the most beautiful eyes?"

Daisy: "A beautiful human?"

Me: "Beekeepers."

Chloe, twirling her hair: "Why beekeepers?"

Me: "Because beauty is in the eye of the beholder."

Daisy: "Good one."

Me: "Whaddaya call a cow after she gives birth?"

Cooper: "Whaddaya Fruit Loops yakking about now?"

Chloe: "Who's a cow?"

Me: "Decaffeinated."

Daisy rolled over laughing.

Me: "Whaddaya call a sleeping cow?"

Chloe: "Binah, stop. Who's a cow?"

Me again: "A bulldozer."

Daisy cackled. "I love it."

Me: "Still on cows. What smells more captivating than the dairy air?"

Daisy was manic: "Nothing. That's hysterical!"

Chloe: "I don't get it."

Me: "Derriere, backside, tushy. Get it?"

Cooper: "You just can't stop, can you?"

Me: "Whaddaya get when you cross an insomniac, an unwilling agnostic, and a dyslexic?"

Chloe: "You're using too many big words."

Me: "You get someone up all night torturing himself mentally over the question of whether or not there's a dog."

Cooper: "Now that's funny." He laughed so hard he peed without lifting his leg.

Me: "That joke belongs to David Foster Wallace."

Cooper: "Who's he?"

Me: "A brilliant human writer who loved dogs."

Cooper: "Daisy, your best friend's a whackadoodle."

Me: "I'm not a whackadoodle. I'm a Havanese. Hey, how do crazy dogs get to Starbarks Park?"

Daisy: "How?"

Me: "They take the psycho path."

Cooper: "Enough already."

Me: "Whaddaya call a deer with no eyes?"

Chloe: "Blind?"

Cooper rolling his eyes: "I have no idea."

Me: "Right."

Cooper: "What's right?"

Me: "No idea."

Cooper: "What?"

Me pointing to my eye: "No eye deer."

Daisy: "I'm hungry."

Me: "I got a job at a bakery because I kneaded dough."

Daisy: "No really, Binah. I'm hungry for cheese."

Me: "Dogs are like Swiss cheese."

Cooper: "I love Swiss cheese."

Chloe: "The holes waste space for more cheese."

Me: "Swiss cheese has holes by design, and so do we. Our holes are not mistakes."

Daisy: "That's a disgusting joke."

Me: "It's not a joke. I'm talking about the holes in our character. The holes we can't see."

Daisy: "Huh?"

Me: "Like peeing in the house."

Chloe: "And like chewing my tail until it bleeds?"

Me: "Yup."

Cooper: "Like sucking on socks because I have anxiety?"

Me: "Yes. And like my unhealthy relationship with my negative voice and melon collie. Our holes give us a chance to change for the better."

Chloe: "So holes are good?"

Me: "That's totally up to us."

Daisy: "Is my hunger a hole?"

Me: "No, Daisy. Let's go get something to eat."

43
Javi

SOON AFTER I *DIE* (IT'S OKAY TO USE THIS WORD), IT'S THUNDERING. Mommy calls my name out because I used to be afraid of loud noises. I try to respond, but she won't recognize the signs because she's not present in the moment.

You can't be present in the moment when you're sad.

Mommy gets up from her bed and goes into the spare bedroom. Binah follows her. Against one wall is a white couch that sits on top of a white rug. Hanging above the couch, on each side of the window, are pictures of Binah and me. Against another wall is a dresser that holds many books we had read, including *Pinocchio*, and a TV that showed many movies we had watched, including *Pinocchio*.

I love Pinocchio.

Against a third wall is a glass china cabinet that holds everything but china. On one side sits Mommy's dolls and on the other side sits her most precious possessions: a music box that plays "Love Story," and me.

Yup, me.

She keeps my ashes in a purple box with this photo of me. I love this photo. I think I look very peaceful.

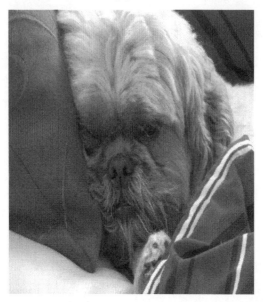

So, it's thundering. Mommy gets the purple box and brings it back to bed with her. She places it on the pillow between her and Binah, kisses my photo, and covers the three of us with the blanket.

"No need to be afraid of the thunder, Javi. Mommy's here."

I wish I could tell her that I'm no longer afraid of anything.

"I miss you, *mi amore*," Mommy kisses my photo again.

Binah kisses my photo, too. "Good night, Javi."

Good night, Binah.

While Mommy sleeps, I tell her that we were meant to be together, even for this short period of time, to help our souls grow. I understand that now.

If only the Rainbow Bridge had visiting hours.

Although I play inside the rainbow, and I've become a part of sunrise and sunset, I still watch over Mommy. I can't be completely free until she's at peace. Sometimes when she's alone, I watch her hold Blue Sweater up to her nose. She cries.

The price of love.

Two months pass like five seconds. Mommy's still sad because her mind focuses on things as they used to be in the past rather than as they are in the present. Why do humans do this?

With her sad eyes, Mommy sits at the dining room table with Binah resting by her feet. She moves around pieces of a jigsaw puzzle. As she puts the final pieces together, I see the puzzle is a photo of me dressed in my tie.

One second frozen in time among a lifetime of seconds.

She stares at this photo. I want so much for her to reach in and pull me out, to brush my hair one last time. It's impossible for me to explain how I feel seeing this lifeless version of me. I'm nostalgic.

Not exactly the word I'm looking for.

I'm sentimental. I'm longing. I'm homesick.

Still not even close.

I'm melancholy.

Yes! That's the word.

In the dusk, in the backyard, Mommy and Binah sit by the pond. It used to be manicured, but now weeds grow between the cracks of the large stones. While the crickets chirp and the frogs croak, Mommy dunks her homemade cookie into her tea and pulls it up. The soggy end falls in. She reaches for another cookie. The plate is covered with a doily.

Doily. That's such a funny word.

Mommy, you'll see, in time you'll laugh again.

That's the problem with humans, they choose to feel sad. They don't realize that spirits are to be celebrated. Mama told me that I fulfilled my purpose. I finished my mission. I was promoted.

Don't humans celebrate promotions?

Mommy touches Binah's face to prove she's real, not an apparition like me, and says, "Do you know what the hardest tea to swallow is?" She takes a sip of her tea while Binah waits for the answer. "Reality, baby girl." She lifts Binah up onto her lap.

Mommy, give it time. Wounds of the soul take longest to heal.

Like a good girl, Binah stays and kisses Mommy's tears.

I have to find a way back to them.

44
Binah

I LOVE THE PICTURE OF JAVI WEARING HIS TIE. HE LOOKED SO handsome despite the photo beginning to fade.

Javi, please tell me this isn't real and that you're coming home.

I'll never forget the dark clouds, mild temperature, and Mommy's painful walk up the driveway as she carefully carried a small purple box. She put it down on the kitchen table as if she were lowering a casket into the hollow, sacred ground.

She whispered, "Binah, Javi's home."

I smelled Javi, but I didn't see him. I paced from room to room, barking, "Javi?" He told me in my dream that he'd be home soon. I barked louder, "JAVI?"

Where are you?

I ran into the bedroom and jumped up onto his favorite striped blanket. His scent was painted all over it. I looked around and breathed in his scent.

"JAVI?"

What the heck is going on?

I raced around in circles until I smelled something familiar, something yummy. Cookies! Javi loved that smell. I raced into the kitchen but found only Mommy. She was baking again.

Javi, where are you?

I waited in the kitchen for him or a cookie. Neither came.

I witnessed Mommy's emotional roller coaster ride. When the hurt left, the anger took its place, and the second anger checked out, loneliness checked in. Mommy muttered long-winded words that went on and on until she ran out of breath. By the end, only her crying was clear.

I sensed her grief. I bowed down. I delivered chew toys. I even presented Allie Gator at her feet. The grand finale was a game Javi taught me. Peekaboo. This game can be equally fun for humans as it is for dogs. I put on my heavy pom-pom sweater, the one with the hood. Yes, I did it by myself. I'm a big girl. And, yes, it was a warm September day, but it was the worst of times.

I was happy to be the joker and desperate to make Mommy laugh. I pulled the hood over my eyes and barked, "Hey, Mommy, where's Binah?"

Within seconds I popped out, "Here I am!"

I'll never forget the sound of Mommy's laughter.

While playing this game with Javi, I learned that I didn't have to see him to know that he was still there. I knew he was still here now. I wish I could explain this to Mommy.

45
Binah

ABOUT A WEEK LATER, I SAT BY THE WINDOW AND WATCHED Mommy walk up the driveway carrying another small package. Once inside, she opened the bag, took out a little tree, and with a trace of a smile whispered, "Binah, Javi's home."

I'm team Mommy all the way, but I now worried that the team captain was about to jump ship.

Mommy said, "Some people make a donation in their dog's honor. We did that. Others get permanent ink, maybe with their dog's name or picture. We did not and will not do that."

Mommy, you're funny. I love how you say 'we,' like I'd actually get a tattoo.

"And others plant a tree. That's us. We're going to plant a tree so Javi's legacy will live on for years to come." Outside, in the backyard, Mommy said, "Binah, pick a special spot where you and your friends will never pee."

I quickly ran over to the pond.

Mommy said, "Where we plant is very important. We can have the most amazing tree, but if we plant in poor soil it's not going to reach its full potential."

I dug my paws into the earth by the highest waterfall, before it branched off into the two smaller ones. "Right here, Mommy!"

"Thank you, Binah." Mommy dug her paws into the dirt until it was deep enough to plant Javi's tree. "Each day that passes, we'll watch this beautiful tree grow big and strong. As long as we think about Javi, we keep him alive. He lives in our hearts."

I refuse to believe that Javi's never coming back home.

Mommy gathered stones and arranged them neatly around the tree in a simple design like she was decorating a cake. "Love hurts," she said.

Am I the only one who can still hear Javi's voice?

"Nay, nay," I heard Javi say. "Only sadness, fear, hate, anger, loneliness, jealousy, envy, and rejection hurt. Love is the only thing that doesn't hurt. Love heals."

I wish Mommy could hear him.

46
Javi

AM I SLEEPING?

"You no longer need sleep," says the Light.

Did I see Santa Claus and his elves?

"They only exist on Earth. You saw angels."

Okay. That makes sense.

My first thought is to wish for the past to return, to search for a dandelion with its yellow flower, puff ball, and dispersing seed. I miss home where I felt the sun, saw the moon, and reached for the stars. I'm now a part of the sun, moon, and stars. My next thought is to ignore my first thought. I am present in the moment. I'm home.

The Light says, "You have waited a lifetime for free will."

Yes, I have.

"In this lifetime, you were given a specific number of chances to change. Because you have made an extra effort to overcome your negative thoughts, you now have the opportunity to advance to a higher level. Do you understand?"

I understand. I'll be responsible for the choices I make.

"You now get to make your first choice. Do you want to watch over Tali from afar, or do you prefer to be the soul that enters her unborn child?"

That's so easy. I can see Mommy and Binah in the future. They're so happy. I want to be with them.

"Careful. Nothing truly worthwhile is easy. If you choose the latter, you are likely to forget everything about your previous lifetime, including Tali and Binah."

But I'll get to be with them again.

"Living life as a human is more than having a body. You will have responsibility. For example, each of your two nostrils will serve a distinct heavenly function. One will carry the spiritual essence of air to your brain, while the other will carry the spiritual

199

essence of air to your heart. The goal is to ensure that your actions are both wise and loving."

I understand.

"What do you understand?"

I understand that humans have the responsibility to love and respect their bodies and souls, and to not abuse them with too much or too little of anything.

"What else do you understand?"

As a human, it's my responsibility to discover my purpose so that I can make Your world a better place.

"Thank you."

I'll take the lessons of unconditional love and obedience I learned in my past life and use them in my next life to learn more lessons.

"It will be challenging at times, but I am here for you."

You always were, are, and will be here for me.

"You will become my cocreator. You will have a lifetime to create yourself in my image. While you are in the womb, you will see all the secrets of the universe, all of your past life experiences and, most importantly, the various moments of transformation you need to achieve during your next lifetime as a human. However, to preserve your free will, an angel will erase your memory of everything you have learned. Embrace the challenges and enjoy your search for meaning."

I send Binah a message.

Get ready. I'm coming home.

47
Binah

Rain or shine, Mommy snapped on my leash. Two seconds outside, I saw the black sky and smelled the thunder around the corner. Two feet out the door, after I squatted and let it all out, I did the hokey-pokey hoping to go right back inside.

Nope.

Mommy opened up the big umbrella. "Let's walk, Binah."

With zero enthusiasm, I scurried along, wearing my new pink-striped raincoat. Trust me, this miniature, four-armed slicker for dogs wasn't a fashion statement. My friends weren't gathering in the street asking, "Where'd your mom get that?"

Daisy's house was on the main road where we walked. With my tail curled under my body and my head tucked inside my hood, I prayed that she wasn't sitting by the window.

"Hey, Binah."

Ugh.

"Hi, Daze."

"I'm in time out."

"What'd ya do now?" I admit I laughed insensitively.

"I peed in the house."

She must've had a setback because she was doing so well.

"Hi, Daisy," Mommy said in her whimsical voice, as she picked up the pace. The raindrops were falling more frequently.

"Daisy, what happens when you get a bladder infection?"

"What'd ya say, Binah?"

"Urine trouble."

"What? I can't hear you."

"Urine trouble."

"Say it again."

"Never mind."

What a waste of a good joke.

"Bye, Bean."

"Bye, Daze."

Nearly three-quarters of a mile into our walk, I saw Cooper resting on the other side of his screen door. By now the rain was really coming down, and together with the strong winds, Mommy's umbrella was no longer enough to keep us dry.

Cooper chuckled. "Better hurry home, Dorothy, and take your little dog, Toto, too."

"That's pretty funny, Cooper," I barked cheerfully.

"What'd ya do today?" he barked through the screen door.

"I tried to catch some fog, but mist."

"Clever."

"What about you?" I asked.

"I'm getting ready to bury my sock."

"That's fantastic, Cooper. Congratulations."

"That's an interesting rain jacket you've got on. Since when do you wear stripes?"

"I didn't want to be spotted."

"Very funny."

The heavy rain dwindled to sprinkles as we approached home. Mommy pointed and said, "Look, Binah, a double rainbow."

Two rainbows.

I knew Mommy was thinking of Javi. I wondered if Javi missed the rain and the comforts of home: Mommy, me, Allie Gator, and Blue Sweater. Although we no longer slept with Javi's picture, Mommy still said good night to him. I understood.

I miss you, too, Javi. I'll always miss you.

48
Javi

SOME THINGS CAN'T BE UNSEEN OR UNFELT.

I enter a kaleidoscope of rich, vivid colors. It's peaceful. No beginning, and seemingly, no end. I'm disconnected from my internal compass, yet I'm not lost. Angels, with their golden halos, hover around me. One angel tells me that death is not the end. Life continues. I will see my family again and again.

We are all heavenly beings.

Another angel tells me that life on Earth is a game. "You get many chances to spin the dial and change the direction of your life. Sometimes you choose the wrong path, but if you're patient and wait your turn to spin again, you get another chance to experience a happy ending."

There are many Once upon a Lifetimes.

I see a double rainbow. Not one, but two rainbows.

Once upon a lifetime, I see two rainbows.

204

49
Binah

MOMMY NAMED MY TOYS.

"Where's Ducky?"

I went and got Ducky.

"Can Ducky sing?"

I squeezed Ducky until the squeal came out of it.

"Where's Teddy Bear?"

Here he is!

"Where's Alligator?"

Oh no, not Allie Gator. I'm not worthy enough.

"Binah, go get Alligator."

I can't.

"Javi would want you to play with his favorite toy."

Really?

"Really, Binah. Go get Alligator."

And the moment I got Allie Gator, something changed. I allowed Allie Gator to comfort me, calm my nerves, and empower me. I could choose to stop the negative thoughts, and, eventually, they'd go away. I had finally learned that my thoughts are like seeds; the more I feed them, the more they grow. I became more mindful to plant happy seeds. I practiced thinking positive thoughts so that I wouldn't wake up melon collie.

I'll have to practice positive thinking every day.

Javi taught me that climbing steps got easier when I practiced climbing them.

It's true. Climbing the steps is now second nature to me.

Practice. Practice. Practice.

Javi was still my hero.

He'll always be my hero.

My friends also changed: Daisy finally learned mind over bladder and stopped peeing indoors. Chloe learned to twirl her hair instead of chew it, and Cooper finally buried his security sock.

Even Mommy changed. One day she was sitting on the stoop with her elbows on her knees, fists under her chin just waiting for time to pass by. I sat with her wishing for a way to turn back time even though it kept ticking on. And the next day the phone rang. I definitely didn't see this coming.

Mommy answered. "Hello?"

Nothing.

"Speaking."

More nothing.

"Yes," Mommy's entire face lit up.

Who in the world are you talking to?

"That's terrific news."

What's terrific news?

"Thank you. Of course, I'll wait."

Wait for what?

Silence.

Hello? Wait for what?

"A boy?"

A boy?

"That's terrific news. I can't thank you enough."

Are we getting a puppy?

"Thank you."

What in the world are you so thankful for?

I clung to Allie Gator to smell Javi. Although time had its way of fading memories, like bright colors fade in hot water, that time still hadn't come.

Javi, where are you? Please give me a sign that you're okay. I want to know when you're coming home.

50
Binah

THE YEAR IS 2014. IT'S A SUNNY DAY IN JULY. LOTS OF HUMANS and dogs stand, sit, and run around in the backyard under the big tent, on the deck, and by the pond. Rainbow-colored balloons soar everywhere.

My best friends and cousins are here with their humans: Daisy, Cooper, Chloe and her new brother Jake, Coco, Annabelle, Cody, Pluto, Molly, Maisie, Riley, and Abby. Javi's first mom and dad are here with their three kids, and so is Dr. Noah.

I'm telling you the place is hopping.

Despite all the fun we dogs can have with the balloons, we choose to hang around the small- to medium-size humans. They're very generous in sharing their food.

Daisy starts a rumor: "Don't eat the green thing."

Chloe: "Don't eat the green thing."

Jake: "Don't eat the green thing."

Cooper, utterly confused asks, "Why?"

Jake turns to his sister, Chloe, who turns to Daisy: "Why?"

Daisy: "It's spoiled."

Chloe turns to Jake who turns to Cooper: "It's spoiled."

Cooper: "Binah, the green thing's spoiled. Don't eat it."

Me: "It's not spoiled. It's sour. It's a sour pickle."

Coco: "Then I can eat it?"

Me: "Yes, Coco. You can eat it."

I get chicken from Erika and Dana, pizza from Seth and Melanie, and Kobe brisket from Grampaw. I share everything with my friends and cousins. Gramma tries to feed me something, but it smells like my friends in the pond. I reject it and quickly run to make sure all the fish are there.

They are.

On the deck, Mommy sits under a big umbrella with my adopted baby brother, Javier. He sits in a highchair made for little humans. Mommy says he weighs twenty pounds. That's less than I weigh. I'm nearly three and a half years old and I weigh twenty-two pounds. I'm a big girl. The big humans are all oohing and aahing over Javier. Mommy smiles as she dips a spoon into a small jar and takes out orangey stuff. It smells decent.

I'll try it.

I walk closer, but the spoon travels above Mommy's head.

"Choo-choo. Here it comes," Mommy says. "Choo-choo."

I sit and open my mouth, but the spoon "choo-choos" right into Javier's mouth.

Mommy says, "I see another tooth coming in, Javier."

With his cheeky, gummy smile, Javier waves to me—me!

"Whaddaya call a toothless bear?" I bark laughing.

My friends and cousins laugh because laughter is contagious, not because they know the joke.

As Javier stirs in his highchair, Mommy's more enthusiastic and curious about the joke than I expect. "What, sweetheart?"

"A gummy bear," I burst out. I'm hysterical, rolling over on the deck, jumping off the deck, rolling over on the grass, and jumping back up onto the deck. My friends and cousins laugh like a bunch of hyenas. Clearly, I've still got it. "Get it, toothless? Gummy?" I laugh so hard that I fart and jump away because I'm so embarrassed that I fart in front of the kid. My friends and cousins cackle and snort. I know I just provided them with enough laughter to last a long time.

Javier laughs, too. At first, I think he's clearing his throat, then I think he's coughing. His hands hit the plastic table in front of him as if he's playing a drum roll for another fart. Everyone's laughing. Humans, big and small, approach from here, there, and everywhere asking, "What's so funny?"

Mommy laughs. "Javier, yes, Binah farted. That's so funny."

Wait. What? You're laughing at me?

"Binah, you are so precious." Mommy puts Javier down, and he waddles on the wooden deck like a drunken sailor. He heads over to my outdoor toy chest. Out of all the toys to grab he chooses Allie Gator.

I whimper, "Please don't take that. That belongs to Javi, pronounced *JA-vee*. You're Javi, pronounced *HA-vee*."

Javier shows me his thumb. "Tum," he smiles at me, sticks out his tongue and licks Allie Gator.

With my eyes as wide as Mommy's smile, I see it.

I hear Mommy say, "No, no, Javier. Phoo-phoo."

I know this is beyond logic. It's a miracle.

I whisper, "Ja-vee?"

"Woof," Javier says as he sticks out his tongue again, displaying a magnificent heart-shaped birth mark on its tip.

I stop trying to find logic where there is none. The only thing I can do is believe.

"Javi! Javi! Javi!" I bark superfast.

Mommy's also excited. "Yes, Javier. That was doggy Javi's favorite toy."

From Javier's little mouth, everyone hears baby talk—the sighs, coos, and cahs—but I hear something very different.

We are all masterpieces to God. He creates each of us with our own unique superhero power to achieve greatness. We all must be nurtured and loved unconditionally. Only then will we be able to express our genius through our writings, art, music, inventions, sports, leadership, and kindnesses.

"Javier." Mommy picks him up. "My precious little man."

I bark, "Mommy, it's Javi!"

"Binah, do you know who my favorite little girl is?"

"ME! I am!" My heart and tail race a thousand beats per minute.

"Yes, Binah. You are such a good girl. You are beautiful, you are funny, and you are so smart. I love you to pieces."

211

Oh, how I love to hear those words. They never get old.

"And do you know who my favorite little boy is?"

She knows.

"Javier!" I bark with confidence.

Mommy knows!

I'm so excited. I kiss Mommy and then Javi and then Mommy and then some random human's leg. This is more than a birthday party for a one-year-old. This is Javi's homecoming and coming home party.

Mommy says, "Welcome home, Javier."

There's singing and there's cake, a lot of cake. Mommy baked gigantic Superboy and Superdog cakes. The cakes are bigger than I am, and I'm a big girl. Everyone gathers around me to open the presents. Javier gets a blue sweater and lots of clothes. We get lots of toys: a glove, a bat, and some nice human gives me a squeaky ball-ball. Gramma and Grampaw give us an envelope with money. How's that fun? They also give us Superboy and Superdog books. Yay! I get a Superdog dress that Mommy puts on me right away.

Mommy says to Javier, "This present is from Binah." She opens up a box that has the bottom half and the top half wrapped separately. She lifts the top half off, ruffles through the tissue paper, and takes out a Superman T-shirt.

Wow. I got him that?

Mommy slips it over Javier's head.

"Where's the cape?" someone calls out.

"Not all superheroes wear capes," Mommy says.

My favorite superhero of all time is my brother, Javi.

There's one present left to unwrap. It's huge. It's the biggest present I've ever seen. It's from Mommy. I know what it is. I've known for a while now, but Mommy told me it was a surprise so I didn't tell anyone, not even Daisy.

"Look, Javier," Mommy says with excitement.

Javier rips the last piece of paper off and shouts, "Car!"

Daisy pushes her way through the crowd. Her eyes widen. She barks with excitement, "Oh my God! Oh my GOD! OH MY GOD!"

This silver car is big enough for Javier to sit down in, yet small enough for his little feet to touch the pedals. Mommy puts him down in the driver's seat. He's a natural.

Humans are similar to cars; they have blind spots. Dogs see what humans overlook. Something in our make-up allows us a millisecond head start to notice motion before humans do. That's why we react before humans see that there's something to react to.

Javier pedals five feet away and stops right next to the praying mantis in front of the pond. Javi's memorial tree, now two-feet tall, is surrounded by dandelions. Am I the only one paying attention? The spherical ball of seeds, with its fluffy attachments, scatter with the faintest breeze. Am I the only one who feels the breeze?

Javi taught me that dandelions are magical flowers, and he showed me how to blow, blow, blow like the wind. But I don't need to make a wish. I have everything I desire.

Grampaw laughs. "Look at the license plate."

My eyes rotate back and forth from the praying mantis to my little brother's smile.

From many voices I hear, "Adorable."

Gramma says, "What does it say?"

"Mitsushihtzu." Mommy laughs. "Mitsushihtzu."

If this were the ending of a movie, here is where the camera would zoom in on my face, and I would say, "In all great fairy tales there's always a plotline where some dog goes beyond his perceived limitations. You don't have to be a superhero in order for your dreams to come true. You just need the courage to break free from your comfort zone. It's the only road to happily ever after."

Love,

Binah

EPILOGUE
Javier

I'VE BEEN TOLD MORE THAN ONCE THAT I'M AN *OLD SOUL*. THESE words have never meant anything to me, at least not until today, July 23, 2029. It's my sixteenth birthday. I was born on the exact month and day, but two years after Javi passed away.

I don't believe in coincidences.

Although chocolate cake is my favorite, Mom bakes a plain vanilla one because I want Binah to have some. She's now eighteen years old, plus five months and one day.

She looks up at me. I feel her adoration.

There are sixteen candle flames, plus one for good luck, dancing in the faint breeze. I know this is an important wish to make. I look at Binah who sits quietly by my side. I believe I can read her mind.

She smiles. *Make it a good one.*

I give Binah the thumbs-up sign and close my eyes.

Dear God, I've known Binah all of my life. The love I feel for her is immeasurable. I know she's slipping away. I can feel it. My wish is for Binah to somehow return to me like I returned to her and Mom. Whatever Your will. Amen.

With my eyes still closed and my very important wish made, I blow, blow, blow like the wind.

I smell Mom's stress hormones as she drives as fast as she can. I believe the red lights are slowing us down for a reason. In the back seat, I cradle Binah on my lap while she cuddles an old, familiar toy. Its vibrant shades of blues and yellows have faded after so many rinse cycles, and its squeal is long gone.

I believe I hear Binah whisper, *I love you, Allie Gator.*

We both inhale its memorable scent.

"Binah?"

Binah glances up at me.

I can't speak. My words are gone.

She kisses Alligator. I instinctively move Binah even closer to me. Her gray silky hair rests against her delicate body and gentle curls cover her underbelly. Her tail is still a feather of soft white fur, and she still has a slight fold in her chin, like a dimple on a human. Binah smiles and shows me her Chiclet teeth. She's missing only one tooth.

Tears well up in my eyes. I choke on my words, "Binah, please keep me in the loop."

Keep you in the loop? You are the loop! You weaved the loop that harnessed me all these years.

"Hey, Binah?"

She slightly lifts her head.

Yeah?

With my index finger gently caressing her back, I trace Binah's visible heart-shaped birthmark. Inside my closed mouth, I glide my tongue, with its hidden heart, over my front teeth. "Our matching birthmarks are not an odd fluke, but rather a shared meaningful experience."

She doesn't answer me.

"I love you, Binah."

I love you more.

Mom parks the car, opens the back door, gently lifts Binah up from my lap, and carries her to the entrance of the animal hospital where Dr. Noah is waiting for us.

Inside, Dr. Noah's voice is comforting. "It's okay, Binah. You shouldn't be in any pain."

Javi?

"Yes, Binah."

You're my favorite superhero of all time.

"You're my favorite superhero, too."

You taught me to believe in miracles.

"Binah, a long time ago, a friend of mine gave me this invisible superhero cape. I've never taken it off, and I believe it always protected me throughout my travels. I was told that I would know when to share it. I would be honored to share this cape with you, Binah. You're the best friend any dog or human can ask for."

Binah nods her head. With grace she tilts it forward.

With my fingers trembling uncontrollably, I go through the motions of taking off my invisible cape, placing it over Binah's head, and tying it into a bow around her neck.

"This never comes off, Binah, not until you feel safe and you're ready to share it with someone else. Okay?"

Okay.

"Believing in miracles makes letting go more bearable."

I understand that it's time to let go. I'll see you again, right?

"You bet, Binah." My fingers reach under her paw while my thumb stretches above it and gently closes the grip.

And you'll take care of Mommy?

"You can count on it."

Knock, knock.

"Who's there?"

Atch.

"Atch who?"

God bless you, my brother, Javi.

218

CAST OF CHARACTERS

Leading Little Man   Leading Little Lady   Leading Little Boy

Javi   Binah   Javier

Best Friends Furever

Elvis   Misty   Ali

Daisy   Chloe   Cooper

Best Cousins Furever (age)

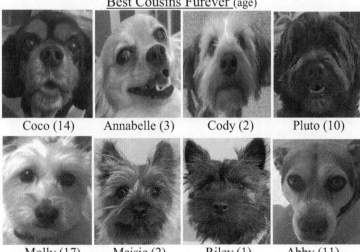

Coco (14)   Annabelle (3)   Cody (2)   Pluto (10)

Molly (17)   Maisie (2)   Riley (1)   Abby (11)

Great Friends

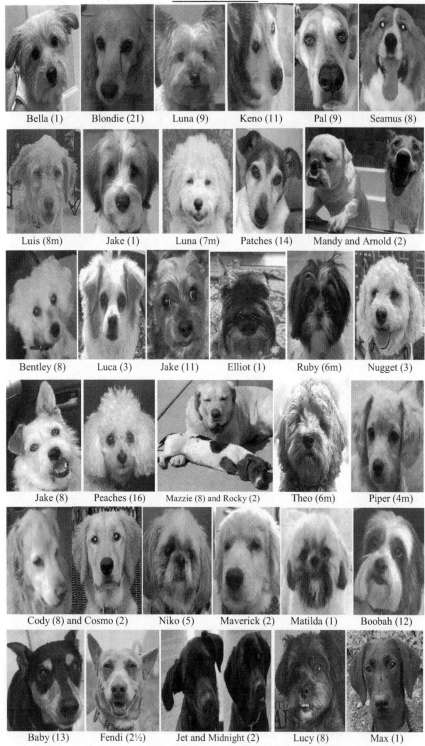

Bella (1)   Blondie (21)   Luna (9)   Keno (11)   Pal (9)   Seamus (8)

Luis (8m)   Jake (1)   Luna (7m)   Patches (14)   Mandy and Arnold (2)

Bentley (8)   Luca (3)   Jake (11)   Elliot (1)   Ruby (6m)   Nugget (3)

Jake (8)   Peaches (16)   Mazzie (8) and Rocky (2)   Theo (6m)   Piper (4m)

Cody (8) and Cosmo (2)   Niko (5)   Maverick (2)   Matilda (1)   Boobah (12)

Baby (13)   Fendi (2½)   Jet and Midnight (2)   Lucy (8)   Max (1)

More Great Friends

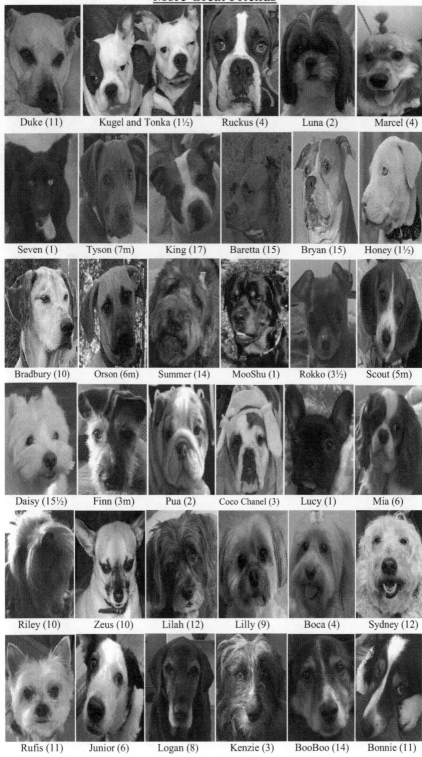

Duke (11) Kugel and Tonka (1½) Ruckus (4) Luna (2) Marcel (4)

Seven (1) Tyson (7m) King (17) Baretta (15) Bryan (15) Honey (1½)

Bradbury (10) Orson (6m) Summer (14) MooShu (1) Rokko (3½) Scout (5m)

Daisy (15½) Finn (3m) Pua (2) Coco Chanel (3) Lucy (1) Mia (6)

Riley (10) Zeus (10) Lilah (12) Lilly (9) Boca (4) Sydney (12)

Rufis (11) Junior (6) Logan (8) Kenzie (3) BooBoo (14) Bonnie (11)

May We All Have This Many Great Friends

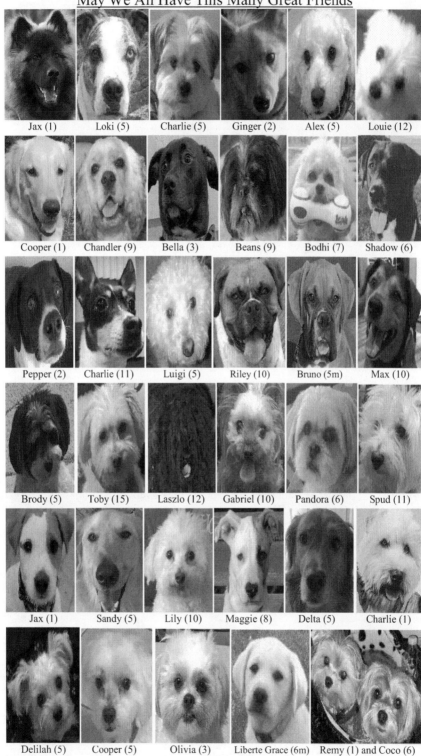

Jax (1)   Loki (5)   Charlie (5)   Ginger (2)   Alex (5)   Louie (12)

Cooper (1)   Chandler (9)   Bella (3)   Beans (9)   Bodhi (7)   Shadow (6)

Pepper (2)   Charlie (11)   Luigi (5)   Riley (10)   Bruno (5m)   Max (10)

Brody (5)   Toby (15)   Laszlo (12)   Gabriel (10)   Pandora (6)   Spud (11)

Jax (1)   Sandy (5)   Lily (10)   Maggie (8)   Delta (5)   Charlie (1)

Delilah (5)   Cooper (5)   Olivia (3)   Liberte Grace (6m)   Remy (1) and Coco (6)

You Can Never Have Too Many Great Friends

Charlie Bear (1) Barrett (6) Louie (12) Isabella (5m) Millie (3m) Cokiti (15½)

Lady (11) Dewi (6) Thor (7) Jake (6) Sadie (2) Leo (10)

Ming (12) Harrison (7) Jett (7) Molly (5) Snow (4) Daschie (10)

Beaux (12) Rosie (2) Princessa (5) Penny (1) Mozy (7m) Buca (5)

Farley (13) Izzy (7) Molly (3) Maddie (13) Koda (2) Dylan (13)

Sophie (2) Jack (13) Maxie (2) Ollie (10) Jojo (7) Lola (1)

Friends on Facebook's "LIFE IS SHORT…GET A DOG"

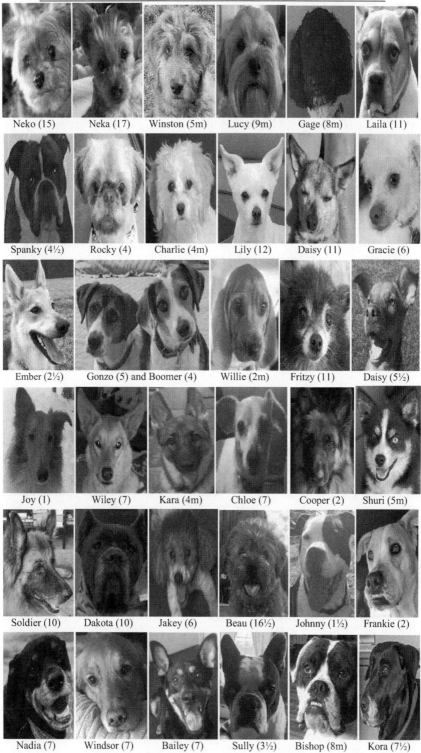

Neko (15)   Neka (17)   Winston (5m)   Lucy (9m)   Gage (8m)   Laila (11)

Spanky (4½)   Rocky (4)   Charlie (4m)   Lily (12)   Daisy (11)   Gracie (6)

Ember (2½)   Gonzo (5) and Boomer (4)   Willie (2m)   Fritzy (11)   Daisy (5½)

Joy (1)   Wiley (7)   Kara (4m)   Chloe (7)   Cooper (2)   Shuri (5m)

Soldier (10)   Dakota (10)   Jakey (6)   Beau (16½)   Johnny (1½)   Frankie (2)

Nadia (7)   Windsor (7)   Bailey (7)   Sully (3½)   Bishop (8m)   Kora (7½)

More Friends on Facebook's "LIFE IS SHORT…GET A DOG"

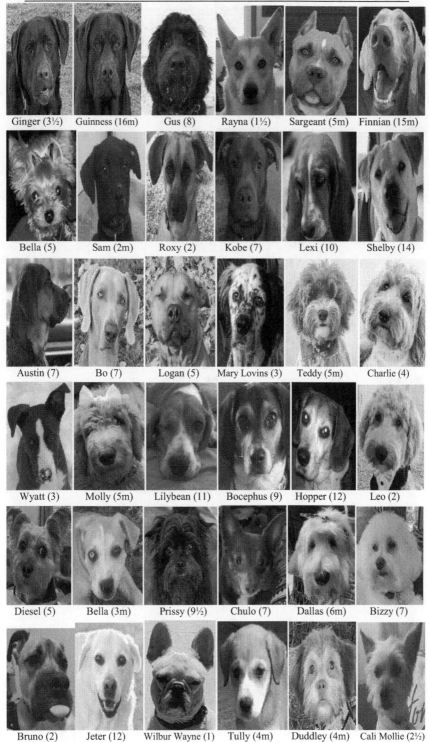

Ginger (3½) Guinness (16m) Gus (8) Rayna (1½) Sargeant (5m) Finnian (15m)

Bella (5) Sam (2m) Roxy (2) Kobe (7) Lexi (10) Shelby (14)

Austin (7) Bo (7) Logan (5) Mary Lovins (3) Teddy (5m) Charlie (4)

Wyatt (3) Molly (5m) Lilybean (11) Bocephus (9) Hopper (12) Leo (2)

Diesel (5) Bella (3m) Prissy (9½) Chulo (7) Dallas (6m) Bizzy (7)

Bruno (2) Jeter (12) Wilbur Wayne (1) Tully (4m) Duddley (4m) Cali Mollie (2½)

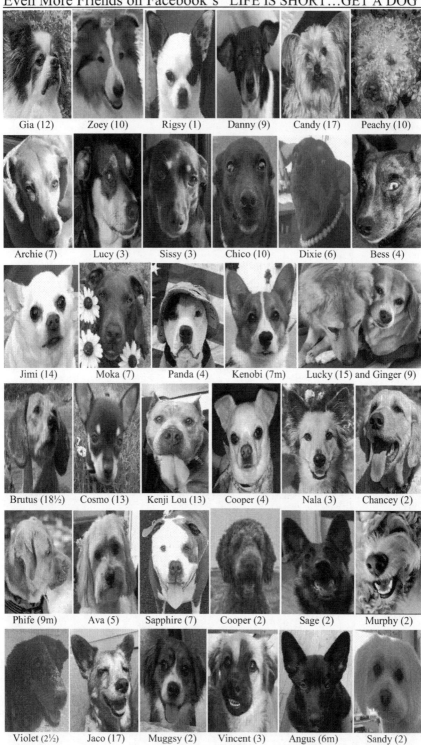

Gia (12)   Zoey (10)   Rigsy (1)   Danny (9)   Candy (17)   Peachy (10)

Archie (7)   Lucy (3)   Sissy (3)   Chico (10)   Dixie (6)   Bess (4)

Jimi (14)   Moka (7)   Panda (4)   Kenobi (7m)   Lucky (15) and Ginger (9)

Brutus (18½)   Cosmo (13)   Kenji Lou (13)   Cooper (4)   Nala (3)   Chancey (2)

Phife (9m)   Ava (5)   Sapphire (7)   Cooper (2)   Sage (2)   Murphy (2)

Violet (2½)   Jaco (17)   Muggsy (2)   Vincent (3)   Angus (6m)   Sandy (2)

So Many Friends on Facebook's "LIFE IS SHORT…GET A DOG"

Toby (1)   Boaz (1)   Sasha (12)   Emma (6)   Rowan (15)   Stella (12)

Spot (9)   Max (3)   Popeye (11)   Molly (3)   Mishka (12)   Winston (4½)   Remi (6)

Hera (2)   Lulu (23)   Spud (20)   Stewie (15)   Spanky (4½)   Jaxson (8m)

Gunther (2)   Jake (8m)   Frannie (2)   Schatzie (3)   Spanky (2m)   Destiny (8m)

Boomer(4)/Doogie(3m)   Rosie (12)   Abbie (4)   Bailey (3)   Truman (7)   Darla (2)

Cambo (2)   Carli (10)   Penelope (12)   Booger (4)   Nuggie (17½)   Zoe (4m)

Maximus (3)   Diva (14)   Yogi (10)   Shayna (4)   Sheldon (10)   Miss Tish (8)

Parker (15)   Harley (7)   Sky (7)   Holly (12)   Murph (6)   Maverick (1½)

Leo (2)   Pearl (1)   Ruby (12)   Gracie (3)   Ducati (2)   Kok (11)

Joey (1)   Frenchie (13)   Charlotte (4)   Monkey (5)   Bosco (10)   Mayo (9)

Tonto (1)   Bailey (2)   Harlee Belle (2)   Daisy (14)   Riley (3)   Roxie (6)

Ducky (10)   Almond Joyelle (3)   Buster (11)   Nova (2½)   Daisy (7)   Rylee May (3)

Thank You Friends From All Over

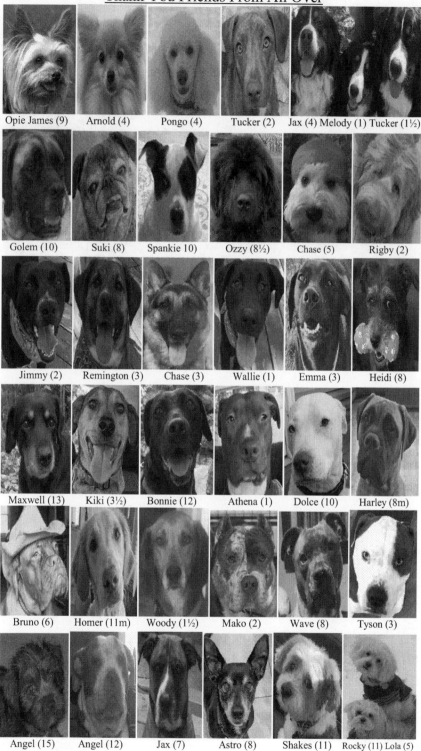

Opie James (9) Arnold (4) Pongo (4) Tucker (2) Jax (4) Melody (1) Tucker (1½)

Golem (10) Suki (8) Spankie 10) Ozzy (8½) Chase (5) Rigby (2)

Jimmy (2) Remington (3) Chase (3) Wallie (1) Emma (3) Heidi (8)

Maxwell (13) Kiki (3½) Bonnie (12) Athena (1) Dolce (10) Harley (8m)

Bruno (6) Homer (11m) Woody (1½) Mako (2) Wave (8) Tyson (3)

Angel (15) Angel (12) Jax (7) Astro (8) Shakes (11) Rocky (11) Lola (5)

Thank You Friends From All Over

Max (1) Ollie (10) Mink (1) Jessie (1) Loonie (11) Mia (15½)

Suri (8) Scarlett (13) Molly (11) Cody (11) Gypsy (14) Ozzy (12) Izzy (7) Fritzy (8) Polar (5)

Jade (2) Finn (10m) May (6m) Maggie-Mae (2m) Chewy (11) Disney (2)

Ruby (3) Max (19 ½) Einstein (2) Leila Rose (1) Pita Marie (15) Sergio (14)

Betty (3m) Sofie (12) Ru (6) Sweetie (7) Elton (9m) Emmi (3)

Stryker (2) Daisy (8) Sheldon (6) Ollie and Stella (2) Simon (11½) Tolley (7½)

Thank You Friends From All Over

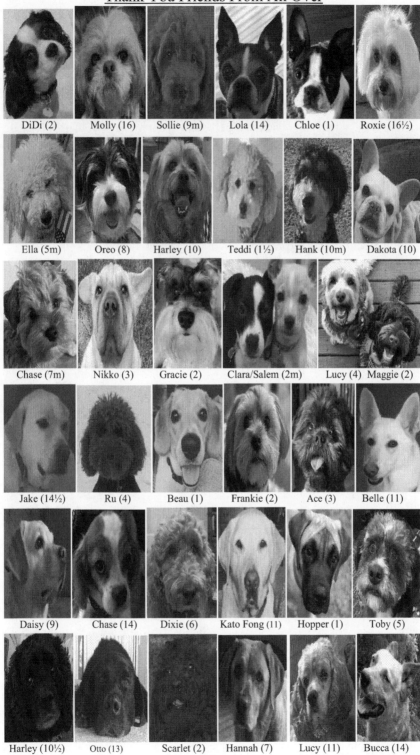

DiDi (2) Molly (16) Sollie (9m) Lola (14) Chloe (1) Roxie (16½)

Ella (5m) Oreo (8) Harley (10) Teddi (1½) Hank (10m) Dakota (10)

Chase (7m) Nikko (3) Gracie (2) Clara/Salem (2m) Lucy (4) Maggie (2)

Jake (14½) Ru (4) Beau (1) Frankie (2) Ace (3) Belle (11)

Daisy (9) Chase (14) Dixie (6) Kato Fong (11) Hopper (1) Toby (5)

Harley (10½) Otto (13) Scarlet (2) Hannah (7) Lucy (11) Bucca (14)

WITH GRATITUDE

Thank you, God. I'm certain there is a reason why man's best friend is your name spelled backward.

Thank you to the Mehta family. Javi changed my life. ♥

ACKNOWLEDGEMENTS

Rich Lehan, I love the book design; thank you for always being on call; Thank you to my on-the-ball copy editor, Adele Brinkley. I look forward to working with you again. Rebecca Graubart, thank you for Binah's photo shoot and the back cover photo.

Thank you to Professors John Hanc and Don Fizzinoglia, and to the students of ProdCo and the Carleton Group at New York Institute of Technology's Communication Arts Dept. for their entertaining and creative book trailer.

Thank you to Tony Wigdzinki and Rallye Motors in Roslyn, NY, for not giving up on finding the Mercedes-Benz toy car for the photo shoot.

A standing ovation for 17-month-old Soli Canle-Carranza, for her debut acting role as Javier; and to Binah, Daisy, Chloe, Cooper, Lily, Teddy, Jax, Dylan, and Maxx for playing so nicely on the day of filming. A special shout out to Dylan Radler and Tyler (Javi's double) for giving us the opportunity to get the photos we needed.

Thank you to: Sara Brenner for your expert legal advice; Sandy Brenner, Stephanie Ewashikor, Phyllis Levine, Carol and Rich Levinson, Caryn Nistico, Marissa Spark, and Barry Stopler for providing great feedback early on; Caryn Albert, Jeannette Falconi, Joseph Della Ferra, Angela Scaturro, Suanne Schafer, Zachary and Gabriel Young, and Linda Zagon for reading an ARC and sharing your reviews on social media.

Thank you Winston and Christopher Gallo, and their Facebook Group, LIFE IS SHORT...GET A DOG, Long Island Dog Parents, and dog lovers everywhere, who shared their dog photos for the paperback edition.

Much love and appreciation to: my fur baby's grandparents, Ceil and Nat; Michael, Barry, Shari and Marina Stopler who love unconditionally; my family who help celebrate every day: Sandy, Norman, Jeffrey, Karen, Sara and Russ; Toby, Herbie, Stephanie, Pam, Brian, Bill, David and Jen.

A shout out to the special little humans in my life (you will always be little to me): Dana, Erika, Melanie, Seth, Eric, Deborah, Elise, Joshua, Zachary, Gabriel, Samantha, Makayla, Colby, Nora, Daniel, Brandon, and Genna. Your precious spirits make me continue to believe in happy endings.

My Brother Javi: A Dog's Tale was named "Finalist" in the 2020 International Book Awards, and is the recipient of the 2020 Pinnacle Book Achievement Award. It also won the Bronze/Third Place Award in the 2021 Feathered Quill Book Awards Program.

"Two astute pooches offer lessons in life, loss, love, and the power of positive thinking. In this novel, readers meet Javi (officially named Java for his café au lait coloring), a purebred Shih Tzu, and Binah, a Havanese whose name means "understanding" in Hebrew. Their vocalizations may be limited to barks, growls, and whimpers, but these two adorable, furry creatures can read and write and frequently wax philosophical. Javi has already crossed the Rainbow Bridge, but he left behind a diary that Binah digs up in the backyard. Binah came into Javi's life only a few months before his death, but she promised him she would tell his story to her friends. Stopler's second novel, whimsical and imaginative, treats readers to the thoughts, pranks, and conversations among these two charmers and their canine friends. Be prepared for chuckles, a bit of magic, and, of course, some tears. Javi was born in 1999 and was fortunate to be able to spend two years with his Mama and his human family—Neha, Roger, and their two young children. But when the humans moved to a new house, much to Javi's distress, they gave Mama away. Still, he learned some important survival lessons from her, most especially how to ignore the negative voice in his head that told him to misbehave—the voice that triggered "melon collie" and always got him into trouble. When Javi was 9 years old, Neha became overworked and stressed. She gave him to Tali, a young woman who once rescued him when he became lost. It was a match made in heaven. Tali and Javi were soul mates. She called him "*mi amore*"; he called her "my lady." Through Tali, Javi found his "mission." Binah joined them as a young pup two years later. In alternating chapters, Binah intersperses her own story, sharing with her friends the wisdom of her beloved "superhero" brother. This enjoyable escapist read for dog lovers, dotted with canine factoids, should also delight youngsters ready to move up to storytime chapter books. The enchanting work delivers a welcome distraction from today's darkness and acrimony. A funny, poignant, and uplifting canine tale." —Kirkus Reviews

To watch the one-minute book trailer Google, *My Brother Javi: A Dog's Tale*
https://www.youtube.com/watch?v=H4G0DeLhx2A

ALSO BY TRACY STOPLER

THE ROPES THAT BIND
ISBN-13: 978-1-53-338111-8

The Ropes That Bind received the 2017 Independent Press Award and the NYC Big Book Award for *Distinguished Favorite* in Women's Fiction. It was also named semi-finalist in the 2018 North Street Prize.

"Debut author Stopler offers a novel, based on a true story, about one woman's struggle to overcome a trauma from her childhood.

"On April 15, 1974, nine-year-old Tali Stark is on her way to school in the Bronx, New York, when a strange man in a white limousine asks her for directions. Tali thinks nothing of stepping into the car, though it's not long before she realizes that she's in danger. The man soon molests her in an empty parking lot before driving her back to school. Young Tali is too afraid to tell anyone about the incident, so she carries the secret in silence for years. Readers follow Tali as she attends high school, graduates from college, falls in love, rediscovers her Jewish roots, and even climbs Mount Kilimanjaro in Tanzania. Through it all, however she remains haunted by the man in the white limousine. The scene of Tali's sexual assault is difficult to read, but the rest of the book moves at a steady clip through the protagonist's life. Throughout, she grows emotionally in ways that are believable, insightful, and tinged with sadness. Her journey through Judaism, for example, provides readers with a crash course in the ideas of cabala, and the details of her therapy sessions show how she faces the disturbing episode of her past. The book paints a strikingly vivid picture of Tali and the challenges she faces on a long, winding road of healing. Rooting for her is easy and watching her mature is endearing, making the novel as a whole a quite memorable experience." —Kirkus Review

To watch the two-minute book trailer Google **The Ropes That Bind Book Trailer**

To watch the 14-minute TEDx talk, Google, **Tracy Stopler TEDx talk**

To order *The Ropes That Bind* on Amazon go to **www.TheRopesThatBind.com**